THE COP,
THE PUPPY
AND ME

THE COP,
THE PUPPY
AND ME

BY

CARA COLTER

First published in Great Britain 2012
by Mills & Boon, an imprint of Harlequin (UK) Limited.
Large Print edition 2012
Harlequin (UK) Limited, Eton House,
18-24 Paradise Road, Richmond, Surrey TW9 1SR

© Cara Colter 2012   0 1 2 4 6 4 4 7 7

ISBN: 978 0 263 22586 0

Printed and bound in Great Britain
by CPI Antony Rowe, Chippenham, Wiltshire

To Rob (again) who loves me through it all.

CHAPTER ONE

OLIVER SULLIVAN—who had been called only Sullivan for so long he hardly remembered his first name—decided he disliked Sarah McDougall just about as much as he'd ever disliked anyone.

And he'd disliked a lot of people.

Meeting dislikable people was a hazard of choosing law enforcement as a profession, not that Ms. McDougall fell into the criminal category.

"Though I have dealt with criminals who were more charming," he muttered to himself. Of course, with criminals he had the advantage of having some authority over them.

All this naked dislike, and Sullivan had yet to even speak to her. His encounters had all been filtered through his voice mail. He'd never seen her, let alone met her, and he would have been only too happy to keep it that way.

But she'd gone to his boss.

Her voice on the phone had been enough to stir his dislike of her and her bulldog-like persistence had cemented it.

Not that her voice was *grating*. It was what she wanted from him that was the problem.

Call me back.

Please.

It's so important.

We have to talk.

Mr. Sullivan, this is urgent.

When he'd managed to totally ignore her, she'd eventually gone to his boss. Sullivan mulled that over with aggravation. Which was worse? The fact that she had gone to his boss? Or the fact that his boss had *ordered* him to comply?

At least go talk to her, the chief had said. *In case you haven't figured it out, you're not in Detroit anymore.*

Oh, Sullivan had figured that out. In about his first five minutes on his new job.

Being a cop in small-town Wisconsin was about as different from being a homicide detective in Detroit as Attila the Hun was different from being Mother Theresa.

"What moment of insanity made me choose Kettle Bend, Wisconsin?" he growled.

Of course his moment of insanity had a name, and her name was Della, his older sister, who had discovered this little pocket of American charm and chosen to come here with her orthodontist husband, Jonathon, to raise her two boys. She'd been trying to convince Sullivan to join their happy family ever since his whole life had gone sideways.

Sullivan shook that off, focused on the town instead. He took in the streets around him with a jaundiced eye.

It looked like the kind of town Walt Disney or Norman Rockwell would have imagined, wide, quiet streets, shaded by enormous trees that he, hard-bitten product of some of Detroit's worst neighborhoods, had no hope of identifying.

Still, there was no missing the newness of the leaves, unfurling in those tender and vibrant shades of spring, the sharp, tangy scent of their newness tickling his nose through his open car window.

Nestled comfortably in the leafy shade were tidy houses, wearing their age and their American flags with equal pride. The houses, for the most part, had a pleasant sameness about them. White with pale yellow trim, or pale yellow with white trim, the odd sage-green and or dove-gray thrown into the mix.

All had deep porches, white picket fences around postage-stamp yards, splashes of spring color in the flower beds lining walkways that welcomed.

But Sullivan refused to be charmed.

He disliked illusions, and he knew this particular illusion to be the most dangerous: that there were places left in the world that were entirely safe and uncomplicated, porch swings and fire-flies, cold lemonade on hot summer afternoons.

That there was a place where doors and windows were unlocked, where children rode their bikes unescorted and unafraid to school, where families laughed over board games. That there were places of unsullied innocence, places that whispered the word *home.* He kept trying to warn Della all was probably not as it appeared.

No, behind the windows and doors of those perfect and pretty houses, Sullivan was willing to bet he would uncover all kinds of secrets that belied the picture he was seeing. Behind some of those closed doors were probably booze bottles hidden down toilet tanks. A kid with a crack problem. Unexplained bruises and black eyes.

It was this cynicism that was making him a poor fit for Kettle Bend.

Certainly a poor fit for Sarah McDougall's plans for him.

Her message on his voice mail chimed through

his head, making him shudder. *We need a hero, Mr. Sullivan.*

He wasn't about to be anybody's hero. This wasn't how he wanted to be spending his day off. He was about to make one Sarah McDougall very, very sorry she'd gone after this bear in his den.

Checking addresses as he went, Sullivan finally pulled over, stepped out of his car and steeled himself against the sleepy appeal of the street he found himself on. On principle, he rolled up his car window and locked his door. The people of Kettle Bend might want to pretend nothing bad ever happened here, but he wasn't going to trust his new car stereo to that notion.

Then he turned to look at the house that sat at 1716 Lilac Lane.

The house differed from its neighbors very little. It was a shingle-sided, single-story bungalow, painted recently—white, naturally—the trim a deep, crisp shade of olive. Vines—he guessed ivy because that was the only name of a vine that he knew—showed signs of new growth, and would shade the wide porch completely in the heat of summer.

Sullivan passed through an outrageously squeaking gate and under an arbor that he knew would drip the color and fragrance of climbing roses in a few more weeks.

He shrugged off the relief it was not happening now, as if there was something about all this charm that was nattering away at his defenses—not like a battering ram, more like an irritating humming, like being pestered by mosquitoes. The scent of roses would have been just one more thing to add to it.

Peripherally, he made note that the concrete walkway was heaved in places, but lined with an odd variety of spring flowers—deep purple, with a starburst yellow interior.

He noticed only because that was what he did.

Sullivan noticed *everything*. Every detail. It made him a great cop. It hadn't helped him be a better human being, as far as he could tell.

He went up the wide stairs to the front door, crossed the shaded porch to it. Before he rang the bell, he studied the outdoor furnishings.

Old wicker chairs, carefully painted the same olive-green as the house trim, held impossibly cheerful plump cushions, with red and yellow and orange flowers in the pattern. Just as the town painted a picture, so did this porch.

A place of rest. Of comfort. Of safety. Of peace.

"Ha," Sullivan snorted cynically, but was aware of setting his shoulders more firmly against the buzzing of all the pesky details working at convincing him he could maybe try letting this woman down softly. He could try being a nice guy.

"Ha," he said again. So far, subtleness had not worked on her. When you phoned a person sixty-two times and they didn't return your calls that did not mean, *Go to the boss.*

It meant, *Get lost. Go away. Find yourself another hero.*

He turned deliberately away from the invitation

of the porch, not prepared to admit for even one small moment, a fraction of a second, that he had imagined himself accepting the invitation.

Rest.

He shook his head, and turned to the door, found the bell—a key type that needed to be turned—and twisted it.

The exterior door was a screen door, white with elaborate carvings around the edges framing the oval of the screen in the middle. The green interior door was open, and he could hear the bell echo through the house.

No one answered, but he figured leaving a door hanging open was an invitation, plain and simple, for prying eyes.

So, unlike the invitation to rest, he took this one, peering in at the house.

The door opened directly into the living room, though a handmade rag rug designated a tiny entry area, and suggested the owner liked order—and wiped feet.

Afternoon sunlight spilled through the open

door and through the picture window, slanting across wood floors that were golden with the patina of age.

Two small couches, a shade of sunshine-yellow that matched the interior of the flowers that marched up the front walk, faced each other over a scarred antique coffee table. Again, there was a sense of order: neatly stacked magazines and a vase of those flowers that had lined the walkway, dipping low on slender stems.

Sullivan had not formed a mental picture of his stalker.

Now he did. Single. No evidence—and there was always evidence—of a man in residence.

No children, because there was no sign of toys or mess, though his eyes caught on a wall of framed magazine covers, hung gallery-style, just inside that front door.

They were all covers from a magazine called *Today's Baby*.

They did nothing to change his initial impression of her. *No life*.

Sullivan was willing to bet the resident of this house was as frumpy as her house was cute. She was no doubt a few pounds too heavy, with frizzy hair and bad makeup, busy making her house look pretty as a picture while she fell into middle-aged decline.

Now that there was nothing left to do on her house—obviously it was magazine photo shoot ready—she'd turned her attention to the town.

Mr. Sullivan, Kettle Bend needs you!

Yeah, right. Kettle Bend needed Oliver Sullivan the way Oliver Sullivan needed a toothache.

He could smell something faintly, drifting through that open door. The scent was sweet. And tart. Home cooking. The sudden, sharp feeling of yearning took him totally by surprise.

He felt it again, like a whisper along his spine. *Rest.*

Again, he shook it off, along with annoying yearnings. He *had* rested. For a whole year. Tying flies and wearing hip waders. It wasn't for him. Too much time for thinking.

Sullivan rang the bell again, impatiently this time.

A cat, a gray puffball with evil green eyes slid out of a hallway, plunked itself in the ray of sunshine and regarded him with slitted dislike, before dismissing him with a lift of its paw and a delicate lick. The cat fit his picture of her life *exactly*.

Still, that cat *knew* he didn't like animals.

Which was what made the whole situation that had gotten him to this front door even more irritating. A hero? He didn't even like dogs. And so he didn't want to answer the question—not from her and not from the dozens of other reporters and TV stations that were hounding him—why he had risked his life for one.

Sullivan gave the handle of the screen door a firm tug, let the door squeak open a noisy inch or two before releasing it to snap shut again.

Come on. An unlocked door?

It made him feel grim. And determined.

This cozy little world was practically begging for a healthy dose of what he had in abundance.

Cynicism.

He backed off the steps and stood regarding the house.

"She's in the back. Sarah's left that rhubarb a bit too long."

Sullivan started. See? It *had* gotten to him. His guard had been down just enough not to notice that his every move was being monitored by the next-door-neighbor. She was a wizened gnome, ensconced in a deep Adirondack chair.

From under a tuft of cotton-ball hair, her bright black marble eyes regarded him with amused curiosity rather than the deep suspicion a stranger *should* be regarded with.

"You're the new policeman," she said.

So, he wasn't a stranger. There was no anonymity in a small town. Not even on your day off, in jeans and a T-shirt.

He nodded, still a little taken aback by how

trust was automatically instilled in him just because he was the new cop on the block.

In Detroit, nine times out of ten, the exact opposite had been true, at least in the hard neighborhoods where he had plied his trade.

"Nice thing you did. With that dog."

Was there one single person on the face of the earth who didn't know? Sullivan was beginning to hate the expression *gone viral* more than any other.

She wouldn't think it was so nice if she knew how often since then he just wished he'd let the damn thing go down the river, raging with spring runoff, instead of jumping in after it.

He thought of it wriggling against him as he lay on the shore of the river afterward, gasping for breath. The puppy, soaked, another layer of freezing on top of his own freezing, had curled up on his exposed skin, right on top of his heart, whimpering and licking him.

Sullivan knew he didn't really wish that he hadn't gone in after it. He just wished that he wished it. And that a person with the cell phone had not recorded his leap into the swollen Kettle River and then posted it on the internet where it seemed the whole world had seen it.

"How is the dog?" she asked.

"Still at the vet," he answered, "but he's going to be fine."

"Has anyone claimed him yet?"

"No."

"Well, I'm sure there will be a long lineup of people who want to adopt him if his owner doesn't show up."

"Oh, yeah," he agreed.

Because of the video, the Kettle Bend Police Department was fielding a dozen calls a day about that dog.

Sullivan followed the narrow concrete path where it curved around the side of the house and then led him down a passageway between houses. Then the path opened into a long, narrow backyard.

There was no word for it.

Except perhaps *enchanting*.

For a moment he stood, breathing it all in: waxy leaves; mature trees; curving flower beds whose dark mounding loam met the crisp edge of freshly cut grass.

There was a sense of having entered a grotto, deeply private.

Sacred.

Sullivan snorted at himself, but a little uneasily this time.

He saw her then.

Crouched beside a fence lined with rows of vigorously growing, elephant-eared plants.

She was totally engrossed in what she was doing, yanking at the thin red stalks of the huge-leafed plants.

It must be the rhubarb her neighbor had mentioned.

She already had a stack of it beside her. Her face was hidden in the shade of a broad-brimmed hat, the light catching her mouth, where her tongue was caught between her teeth in concentration.

She was wearing a shapeless flowered tank top and white shorts, smudged with dirt, but the long line of strong legs, already beginning to tan, took his breath away.

As he watched, she tugged vigorously on one of the plants. When the stalk parted with the ground, she nearly catapulted over backward. When she righted herself, she went very still, as if she knew, suddenly, she was not alone.

Without getting up, she pivoted slowly on the heels of her feet and looked at him, her head tilted quizzically, possibly aggrieved that he had caught her in a wrestling match with the plant.

Sarah McDougall, if this was her, was certainly not middle-aged. Or frizzy-haired. She was wearing no makeup at all. The feeling of his breath being taken away was complete.

Corkscrew auburn curls escaped from under the brim of her hat and framed an elfin face. A light scattering of freckles danced across a daintily snubbed nose. Her cheekbones and her chin mirrored that image of delicacy.

But it was her eyes that threatened to undo him. He was good at this: at reading eyes. It was harder than people thought. A liar could look you straight in the face without blinking. A murderer could have eyes that looked as soft as suede, as gentle as a fawn's.

But eleven years working one of the toughest homicide squads in the world had honed Sullivan's skills to a point that his sister called him, not without a hint of admiration, scary in his ability to detect what was real about a person.

This woman's eyes were huge and hazel, and stunningly, slayingly gorgeous.

She was, obviously, the all-American girl. Wholesome. Sweet. Probably ridiculously naive.

Case in point: she left her door unlocked and wanted to make *him* a hero!

But instead of that fueling his annoyance at her, instead of remembering his fury that she had called his boss, Sullivan felt a surge of foolish protectiveness.

"You should lock your front door when you

work back here," he told her gruffly. Part of him wanted to leave it at that, to turn his back and walk away from her. Because obviously what a girl like that needed to be protected from most was a guy like him.

Who had seen so much darkness it felt as if it had taken up residence inside of him. Darkness that could snuff out the radiance that surrounded her like a halo.

Still, if he left without giving her an opportunity to see that in him, she might pester him, or his boss, endlessly.

So he forced himself to cross the yard until he stood above her, until his shadow passed over the wideness of those eyes.

He rarely shook hands. Keep the barriers up. Establish authority. Don't invite familiarity. Keep your distance.

So it startled him when he wanted to extend a hand to her.

"Sarah McDougall?" he asked, and at her wide-eyed nod, "I'm Sullivan."

The aggrieved look faded from her face. She actually looked thrilled! He was glad he had shoved his hand in his pocket instead of holding it out to her.

"Mr. Sullivan," she said, and scrambled to her feet. "I'm so glad you came. May I call you Oliver?"

"No, you may not. No one calls me Oliver. And it's not Mister," he said, his voice deliberately cold. "It's Officer."

A touch of wariness tinged her gaze. Hadn't she been able to tell from her unanswered pleas that he was a man who deserved her wariness?

"No one calls you Oliver?"

What was she asking that question for? Hadn't he made it eminently clear there was going to be nothing personal between them, not even an invitation to use first names?

"No." His voice had a bit of a snap to it.

Which she clearly did not recognize, or she would have had the sense to back away from the subject.

"Not even your mother?" She raised a skeptical eyebrow. Her looking skeptical was faintly comical, like a budgie bird trying to look aggressive.

"Dead," he snapped. He could see sympathy crowding her eyes, and there was no way he was allowing all that softness to spill out and touch him. His mother had died when he was seventeen years old.

And his father.

Seventeen years ago was a place he did not revisit.

There was no sense her misconstruing his reasons for being here, and there was only one way to approach a person like this.

Brutal bluntness.

"Don't call me anymore," he said, holding her gaze, his voice deliberately low and flat. "I'm not helping you. Not if you call six million times. I'm not any kind of hero. I don't want to be your friend. I don't want to save your town. And don't call my boss again, either. Because you don't want me to be your enemy."

Sullivan saw, astonished at his failure, that his legendary people-reading skills were slightly off-kilter. Because he had thought she would be easily intimidated, that he could make her back down, just like that.

Instead he saw that cute little mouth reset itself in a line that was unmistakably stubborn and that could mean only one thing for him.

Trouble.

Sarah stared up at her unexpected visitor, caught off balance, not just by her tug-of-war with her rhubarb, but also by the fact she'd had a witness to it!

Add to that his unexpected sharpness of tone, his appearance in her yard, his appearance, period, and her feeling of being unbalanced grew.

She'd been totally engrossed in wresting the rhubarb from the ground. Which was what she needed from her house, her yard, her garden and her work.

There was always something that needed to be done, the hard work unending.

But her total focus on what she'd been doing had left her vulnerable. Though Sarah suspected that even if you had been expecting this man, had laid out tea things and put on a presentable dress, the feeling you would have when you experienced the rawness of his presence would be one of vulnerability.

The grainy video she had seen—along with millions of other people—had not really prepared her for the reality of him. Though she had already figured out from her unanswered calls that he was not exactly going to be the kind of guy the heroic rescue of a drowning puppy had her wanting him to be.

From thirty seconds of film, from him ripping off his shirt and jumping into the icy water just past where the Kettle River ran under the bridge in downtown Kettle Bend, to lying on the bank after, the pup snuggled into the pebbled flesh of his naked chest, she had jumped to conclusions.

He was courageous. That much was in his eyes. A man afraid of nothing.

But she had thought—a man willing to risk his life for a dog, after all—that he would be gentle and warm.

If his message on his voice mail had been a touch abrupt, she had managed to dismiss that as part of his professional demeanor. But then the fact that he had not returned her increasingly desperate calls?

And now he had been downright rude to her.

Plus, there was nothing warm in those dark eyes. They were cool, assessing. There was a wall so high in them it would be easier to scale Everest.

Sarah felt a quiver of doubt. The reality of Oliver Sullivan versus the fantasy she had been nursing since she had first seen the clip of him did not bode well for her plan, unless he could be tamed, and from looking at him that seemed highly unlikely!

Sullivan was dressed casually, dark denims,

a forest-green T-shirt that molded the fullness of his chest, the hard mounds of firm biceps. A hundred other guys in Kettle Bend were wearing the same thing today, but she bet none of them radiated the raw potency that practically shivered in the spring sunshine around him.

He looked like a warrior wearing the disguise of a more civilized man.

He was one of those men who radiated a subtle confidence in his own strength, in his ability to handle whatever came up. It was as if he was ready and waiting for all hell to break loose.

Which was so utterly at odds with the atmosphere in her garden that it might have made her smile, except there was something about the stripping intensity of his expression that made her gulp instead.

Despite astonishing good looks, he had the expression of a man unutterably world-weary, a man who expected the absolute worst from people, and was rarely disappointed.

Still, he *was* unnervingly good-looking. If she

could talk him into doing some TV interviews, the camera would love his dark, chocolate hair, short and neat, slashing brows over eyes so dark brown they could have been mistaken for black. He had a strong nose, good cheekbones, wide sensual lips and a devilish little cleft in his chin.

She could not allow herself the luxury of being intimidated by him.

She just couldn't.

Kettle Bend needed him.

Not that she wanted to be thinking of him in the same sentence as the word *need*.

Because he was the kind of man who made a woman aware of things—*needs*—she was sure she had laid to rest.

He was the kind of man whose masculinity was so potent it could make a woman ache for things she had once had, and had no longer. Fevered kisses. Strong arms. Laughter in the night.

He was the kind of man who could almost make a woman entirely forget the terrible price, the pain that you could invite by looking for those things.

Sarah McDougall didn't need anyone looking out for her, thank you very much! It was one of the things she prided herself on.

Fierce independence.

Not needing anyone. Not anymore. Not ever again.

Inheriting this house, and her grandmother's business, Jelly Jeans and Jammies, had allowed her that.

She could *not* back down from him! So, with more confidence than she felt, in defiance of his hostility, she whipped the gardening glove off her hand, wiped it on her shorts just in case, and extended it to him.

Then she held her breath waiting to see if he would take it.

CHAPTER TWO

OFFICER Oliver Sullivan looked at Sarah's extended hand, clearly annoyed at her effort to make some kind of contact with him.

She knew he debated just walking away now that he had delivered his unfriendly message.

But he didn't. With palpable reluctance, he accepted her hand, and his shake was brief and hard. She kept her face impassive at the jolt that surged, instantaneously, from her fingertips to her elbow. It would be easy to think of rough whiskers scraping a soft cheek, the smell of skin out of the shower.

Easy, too, to feel the tiniest little thrill that her life had had this unexpected moment thrust into it.

Sarah reminded herself, sternly, that her life was full and rich and complete.

She had inherited her grandmother's house in this postcard-pretty town. With it had come a business that provided her a livelihood and that had pulled her back from the brink of despair when her engagement had ended.

Kettle Bend had given her something she had not thought she would ever have again, and that she now could appreciate as that rarest of commodities: contentment.

Okay, in her more honest moments, Sarah knew it was not complete contentment. Sometimes, she felt a little stir of restlessness, a longing for her old life. Not her romance with Michael Talbot. No, sir, she was so over her fiancé's betrayal of her trust, *so* over him.

No, it was elements of her old life as a writer on the popular New York–based *Today's Baby* magazine that created that nebulous longing, that called to her. She had regularly met and interviewed new celebrity moms and dads, been invited to glamorous events, been a sought-after guest at store openings and other events. She had loved being creative.

A man like the one who stood in front of her posed a danger. He could turn a small longing for *something*—excitement, fulfillment—into a complete catastrophe.

Sarah reminded herself, sternly and firmly, that she had already found a solution for her nebulous longings; she was going to chase away her restlessness with a new challenge, a huge one that would occupy her completely. Her new commitment was going to be to the little community that was fading around her.

Her newfound efforts at contentment relied on getting this town back to the way she remembered it being during her childhood summers spent here: vital, the streets overflowing with seasonal visitors, a feeling of endless summer, a hopeful vibrancy in the air.

So, handshake completed, Sarah crossed her arms over her chest, a thin defense against some dark promise—or maybe threat—that swirled like electricity in the air around him.

She wanted him to think she was not rattled.

"I have a great plan for Kettle Bend," she told him. She had interviewed some of the most sought-after people in the world. She would not be intimidated by him. "And you can help make it happen."

He regarded her long and hard, and then the tiniest of smiles tickled the corner of that sinfully sensuous mouth.

She thought she had him. Then…

"No," he said. Simple. Firm. Unshakable, the smile gone from the corner of that mouth as if it had never been.

"But you haven't even heard what I have to say!" Sarah sputtered indignantly.

He actually seemed to consider that for a moment, though his deeply weary sigh was not exactly encouraging.

"Okay," he said after a moment, those dark eyes shielded, unreadable. "Spit it out."

Spit it out? As an invitation to communication, it was somewhat lacking. On the other hand, at least he wasn't walking away. Yet. But his body language indicated the thread that held him here, in her yard, was thin.

"The rescue of the dog was incredible. So courageous."

He failed to look flattered, seemed to be leaning a little more toward the exit, so she rushed on. "I've seen it on the internet."

His expression darkened even more—if that was possible—so she didn't add that she had watched it more than a dozen times, feeling foolishly compelled to watch it again and again for reasons she didn't quite understand.

But she did understand that she was not the only one. The video had captured hearts around the world. As she saw it, the fact he was standing in her yard meant that she had an opportunity to capitalize on that magic ingredient that was drawing people by the thousands to that video.

"I know you haven't been in Kettle Bend very

long," Sarah continued. "Didn't you know how cold that water was going to be?"

"If I had known how cold that water was going to be, I would have never jumped in."

That was the kind of answer that wouldn't work *at all* in the event she could talk him into being a participant in her plan to use his newfound notoriety to publicize the town.

Though that possibility seemed more unlikely by the second.

At least he was talking, and not walking.

"You must love dogs," she said, trying, with growing desperation, to find a chink in all that armor.

He didn't answer her, though his chest filled as he drew in a long breath. He ran an impatient hand through the thick, crisp silk of his dark hair.

"What do you want from me?"

Her eyes followed the movement of his hand through his hair, and for a moment the sensation of what she *really* wanted from him nearly swamped her.

Sarah shook it off, an unwanted weakness.

"Your fifteen minutes of fame could be very beneficial to this town," she said, trying, valiantly, and not entirely successfully, not to wonder how his hair would feel beneath her fingertips.

"Whether I like it or not," he commented dryly.

"What's not to like? A few interviews with carefully chosen sources. It would take just the smallest amount of your time," she pressed persuasively.

His look of impatience deepened, and now annoyance layered on top of it. Really, such a sour expression should have made him much less good-looking!

But it didn't.

Still, she tried to focus on the fact that he was still standing here, giving her a chance. Once she explained it all to him, he couldn't help but get on board!

"Do you know what Summer Fest is?" she asked him.

"No. But it sounds perfectly nauseating."

She felt her confidence falter and covered it by glaring at him. Sarah decided cynical was just his default reaction. Who could possibly have anything against summer? Or a festival?

Sarah plunged ahead. "It's a festival for the first four days of July. It starts with a parade and ends with the Fourth of July fireworks. It used to kick off the summer season here in Kettle Bend. It used to set the tone for the whole summer."

She waited for him to ask what had happened, but he only looked bored, raising an eyebrow at her.

"It was canceled, five years ago. The cancellation has been just one more thing that has contributed to Kettle Bend fading away, losing its vibrancy, like a favorite old couch that needs recovering. It's not the same place I used to visit as a child."

"Visit?" It rattled her that he seemed not to be showing the slightest interest in a single word she said, but he picked up on that immediately. "So you're not a local, either?"

Either. A bond between them. *Play it.*

"No, I grew up in New York. But my mother was from here, originally. I used to spend summers. And where are you from? What brings you to Kettle Bend?"

"Momentary insanity," he muttered.

He certainly wasn't giving anything away, but he wasn't walking away, either, so Sarah prattled on, trying to engage him. "This is my grandmother's house. She left it to me when she died. Along with her jam business. Jelly Jeans and Jammies. You might have heard of it. It's very popular around town."

Sarah was not sure she had engaged him. His expression was impossible to read. She had felt encouraged that he showed a slight interest in her. Now, she was suspicious. Sullivan was one of those men who found out things about people, all the while revealing nothing of himself.

"Look, Miss McDougall—"

She noticed he did not use her first name, and knew, despite that brief show of interest, he was keeping his distance from her in every way he could.

"—not that any of this has anything to do with me, but nothing feels or looks the same to an adult as it does to a child."

How had he managed, in a single line, to make her feel hopelessly naive, as if she was chasing something that didn't exist?

What if he was right?

Damn him. That's what these brimming-with-confidence-and-cynicism men did. Made everyone doubt themselves. Their hopes and dreams.

Well, she wasn't giving her hopes and dreams into the care of another man. Michael Talbot had already taught her that lesson, thank you very much.

When she'd first heard the rumor about Mike, her fiancé and editor in chief of *Today's Baby*, and a flirty little freelancer named Trina, Sarah had refused to believe it. But then she had seen them together in a café, something too cozy about the way they were leaning into each other to confirm what she wanted to believe, that Mike and Trina's relationship was strictly business.

Her dreams of a nice little house, filled with babies of her own, had been dashed in a flash.

No accusation, just, *I saw you and Trina today.*

The look of shame that had crossed Mike's face had said it all, without him saying a single word.

Now, Sarah had a replacement dream, so much safer. A town to revitalize.

"Yes, it does have something to do with you!"

"I don't see how."

"Because I've been put in charge of Summer Fest. I've been given one chance to bring it back, to prove how good it is for this town," she explained.

"Good luck with that."

"I've got no budget for promotion. But I bet your phone has been ringing off the hook since the clip of the rescue was shown on the national evening news." She read the answer in his face. "*The A.M. Show, Good Night, America, The Way*

We See It, *Morning Chat with Barb*—they're all calling you, aren't they?"

His arms had now folded across the immense-ness of his chest, and he was rocking back on his heels, watching her with narrowed eyes.

"They're begging you for a follow-up," she guessed. She wasn't the only one who had been able to see that this man and that dog would make good television.

"You'll be happy to know I'm not answering their calls, either," he said dryly.

"I am not happy to know that! If you could just say yes to a few interviews and mention the town and Summer Fest. If you could just say how wonderful Kettle Bend is and invite everybody to come for July 1. You could tell them that you're going to be the grand marshal of the parade!"

It had all come out in a blurt.

"The grand marshal of the parade," he repeated, stunned.

She probably should have left that part until

later. But then she realized, shocked, he had not repeated his out-and-out no.

He seemed to realize it, too. "No," he said flatly.

She rushed on as if he hadn't spoken. "I don't have a hope of reaching millions of people with no publicity budget. But, Oli—Mr.—Officer Sullivan—you do. You could single-handedly bring Summer Fest back to Kettle Bend!"

"No," he said again, no hesitation this time.

"There is more to being a cop in a small town than arresting poor old Henrietta Delafield for stealing lipsticks from the Kettle Mug and Drug."

"Mug and Drug," he repeated dryly, "that sounds like my old beat in Detroit."

Despite the stoniness of his expression, Sarah allowed herself to feel the smallest stirring of hope. He had a sense of humor! And, he had finally revealed something about himself. He was starting to care for his new town, despite that hard-bitten exterior.

She beamed at him.

He backed away from her.

"Let me think about it," he said with such patent insincerity she could have wept.

Sarah saw it for what it was, an escape mechanism. He was slipping away from her. She had been so sure, all this time, when she'd hounded him with message after message, that when he actually heard her brilliant idea, when he knew how good it would be for the town, he would *want* to do it.

"There's no time to think," she said. "You're the hot topic *now*." She hesitated. "Officer Sullivan, I'm begging you."

"I don't like being impulsive." His tone made it evident he *scorned* being the hot topic and was unmoved by begging.

"But you jumped in the river after that dog. Does it get more impulsive than that?"

"A momentary lapse," he said brusquely. "I said I'll think about it."

"That means no," she said, desolately.

"Okay, then, no."

There was something about the set of his shoulders, the line around his mouth, the look in his eyes that he had made up his mind absolutely. He wasn't *ever* going to think about it, and he wasn't *ever* going to change his mind. She could talk until she was blue in the face, leave four thousand more messages on his voice mail, go to his boss again.

But his mind was made up. Like the wall in his eyes, it would be easier to climb Everest than to change it.

"Excuse me," she said tautly. She bent and picked up her rhubarb, as if it could provide some kind of shield against him, and then shoved by him. She headed for the back door of her house before she did the unthinkable.

You did not cry in front of a man as hard-hearted as that one.

Something in his face, as she glanced back, made her feel as if her disappointment was transparent to him. She was all done being vulnerable. Had she begged? She hoped she hadn't begged!

"You should try the Jelly Jeans and Jammies

Crabbies Jelly," she shot over her shoulder at him. "It's made out of crab apples. My grandmother swore it was a cure for crankiness."

She opened her back screen door and let it slam behind her. The back door led into a small vestibule and then her kitchen.

She was greeted by the sharp tang of the batch of rhubarb jam she had made yesterday. Every counter and every surface in the entire kitchen was covered with the rhubarb she needed to make more jam today.

Because this was the time of year her grandmother always made her Spring Fling jam, which she had claimed brought a feeling of friskiness, cured the sourness of old heartaches and brought new hope.

But given the conversation she had just had, and looking at the sticky messes that remained from yesterday, and the mountains of rhubarb that needed to be dealt with today, hope was not exactly what Sarah felt.

And she certainly did not want to think of

all the connotations friskiness could have after meeting a man like that one!

Seeing no counter space left, she dumped her rhubarb on the floor and surveyed her kitchen.

All this rhubarb had to be washed. Some of it had already gotten tough and would have to be peeled. It had to be chopped and then cooked, along with all the other top secret ingredients, in a pot so huge Sarah wondered if her grandmother could have possibly acquired it from cannibals. Then, she had to prepare the jars and the labels. Then finally deliver the finished product to all her grandmother's faithful customers.

She felt exhausted just thinking about it. An unguarded thought crept in.

Was this the life she really wanted?

Her grandmother had run this little business until she was eighty-seven years old. She had never seemed overwhelmed by it. Or tired.

Sarah realized she was just having an off moment in her new life.

That was the problem with a man like Oliver

Sullivan putting in a surprise appearance in your backyard.

It made you question the kind of life you *really* wanted.

It made you wonder if there were some kinds of lonely no amount of activity—or devotion to a cause—could ever fill.

Annoyed with herself, Sarah stepped over the rhubarb to the cabinet where she kept her telephone book.

Okay. He wasn't going to help her. It was probably a good thing. She had to look at the bright side. Her life would have tangled a bit too much with his had he agreed to use his newfound fame to the good of the town.

She could do it herself.

"WGIV Radio, how can I direct your call?"

"Tally Hukas, please."

After she hung up from talking to Tally, Sarah wondered why she felt the tiniest little tickle of guilt. It was not her job to protect Officer Oliver Sullivan from his own nastiness.

* * *

"And so, folks," Sarah's voice came over the radio, in that cheerful tone, "if you can spare some time to help our resurrected Summer Fest be the best ever, give me a call. Remember, Kettle Bend needs you!"

Sullivan snapped off the radio.

He had been so right in his assessment of Sarah McDougall: she was trouble.

This time, she hadn't gone to his boss. Oh, no, she'd gone to the whole town as a special guest on the Tally Hukas radio show, locally produced here in Kettle Bend. She'd lost no time doing it, either. He'd been at her house only yesterday.

Despite that wholesome, wouldn't-hurt-a-flea look of hers, Sarah had lost no time in throwing him under the bus. Announcing to the whole town how she'd had this bright idea to promote the summer festival—namely him—and he'd said no.

Ah, well, the thing she didn't get was that he didn't care if he was the town villain. He would actually be more comfortable in that role than the one she wanted him to play!

The thing *he* didn't get was how he had thought about her long after he'd left her house yesterday. Unless he was mistaken, there had been tears, three seconds from being shed, sparkling in her eyes when she had pushed by him.

But this was something she should know when she was trying to find a town hero: an unlikely choice was a man unmoved by tears. In his line of work, he'd seen way too many of them: following a knock on the door in the middle of the night; following a confession, outpourings of remorse; following that moment when he presented what he had, and the noose closed. He had them. No escape.

If you didn't harden your heart to it all, you would drown in other people's tragedy.

He'd *had* to hurt Sarah. No choice. It was the only way to get someone like her to back off. Still, hearing her voice over the radio, he'd tried to stir himself to annoyance.

He was reluctant to admit it was actually something else her husky tone caused in him.

A faint longing. The same faint longing he had felt on her porch and when the scent from her kitchen had tickled his nose.

What *was* that?

Rest.

Sheesh, he was a cop in a teeny tiny town. How much more restful could it get?

Besides, in his experience, relationships weren't restful. That was the last thing they were! Full of ups and downs, and ins and outs, and highs and lows.

Sullivan had been married once, briefly. It had not survived the grueling demands of his rookie year on the homicide squad. The final straw had been someone inconveniently getting themselves killed when he was supposed to be at his wife's sister's wedding.

He'd come home to an apartment emptied of all her belongings and most of his.

What had he felt at that moment?

Relief.

A sense that now, finally, he could truly give one hundred percent to the career that was more than a job. An obsession. Finding the bad guy possessed him. It wasn't a time clock and a paycheck. It was a life's mission.

He started, suddenly realizing it was that little troublemaker who had triggered these thoughts about relationships!

He was happy when his phone rang, so he didn't have to contemplate what—*if*—that meant something worrisome.

Besides, his discipline was legendary—as was his comfortably solitary lifestyle—and he was not thinking of Sarah McDougall in terms of the "R" word. He refused.

He glanced at the caller ID window.

His boss. That hadn't taken long. Sullivan debated not answering, but saw no purpose in putting off the inevitable.

He held the phone away from his ear so

the volume of his chief's displeasure didn't deafen him.

"Yes, sir, I got it. I'm cleaning all the cars."

He held the phone away from his ear again. "Yeah. I got it. I'm on Henrietta Delafield duty. Every single time. Yes, sir."

He listened again. "I'm sure you will call me back if you think of anything else. I'm looking forward to it. No, sir. I'm not being sarcastic. Drunk tank duty, too. Got it."

Sullivan extricated himself from the call before the chief thought of any more ways to make his life miserable.

He got out of his car. Through the open screen door of Della's house—a house so like Sarah's it should have spooked him—he could hear his nephews, Jet, four, and Ralf, eighteen and half months, running wild. He climbed the steps, and tugged the door.

Unlocked.

He went inside and stepped over an overturned basket of laundry and a plastic tricycle. His sister had once been a total neat freak, her need for order triggered by the death of their parents, just as it had triggered his need for control.

He supposed that meant the mess was a good thing, and he was happy for her, moving on, having a normal life, despite it all.

Sullivan found his sister in her kitchen. The two boys pushed by him, first Jet at a dead run, chortling, tormenting Ralf by holding Ralf's teddy bear high out of his brother's reach. Ralf toddled after him, determined, not understanding the futility of his determination was fueling his brother's glee.

Della started when she turned from a cookie sheet, still steaming from the oven, and saw Sullivan standing in her kitchen door well. "You scared me."

"You told me to come at five. For dinner."

"I lost track of time."

"You're lucky it was me. You should lock the door," he told her.

She gave him a look that in no way appreciated

his brotherly concern for her. In fact, her look left him in no doubt that she had tuned into the Tally Hukas show for the afternoon.

"All Sarah McDougall is trying to do is help the town," Della said accusingly.

Jet raced by, cackling, toy high. Sullivan snagged it from him, and gave it to Ralf. Blessedly, the decibel level was instantly reduced to something that would not cause permanent damage to the human ear.

Sullivan's eyes caught on a neatly bagged package of chocolate chip cookies on the counter. His sister usually sent him home with a goodie bag after she provided him with a home-cooked meal.

"Are those for me?" he asked hopefully, hoping she would take the hint that he didn't want to talk about Sarah McDougall.

His sister had never been one to take hints.

"Not now, they aren't," she said sharply.

"Come on, Della. The chief is already punishing me," he groaned.

"How?" she said, skeptical, apparently, that

the chief could come up with a suitable enough punishment for Sullivan refusing to do his part to revitalize the town.

"Let's just say it looks like there's a lot of puke in my future."

"Humph." She was a woman who dealt with puke on a nearly daily basis. She was not impressed. She took the bagged cookies and put them out of sight. "I'm going to donate these to the bake sale in support of Summer Fest."

"Come on, Della."

"No, *you* come on. Kettle Bend is your new home. Sarah's right. It needs *something*. People to care. Everyone's so selfish. Me. Me. Me. Indifferent to their larger world. What happened to Kennedy? *Think not what your country can do for you, but what you can do for your country?*"

"We're talking about a summer festival, not the future of our nation," he reminded her, but he felt the smallest niggle of something astonishing. Was it *guilt?*

"We're talking about an attitude! Change starts small!"

His sister was given to these rants now that she had children and she felt responsible for making good citizens of the world.

Casting a glance at Jet, who was using sweet talk to rewin his brother's trust and therefore get close to Bubba the bear, Sullivan saw it as a monumental task she had undertaken. With a crow of delight, Jet took the bear. She obviously had some way to go.

If she was going to work on Sullivan, too, her mission was definitely doomed.

"Why on earth wouldn't you do a few interviews if it would help the town out?" Della pressed him.

"I'm not convinced four days of summer merriment *will* help the town out," he said patiently. "I haven't been here long, but it seems to me what Kettle Bend needs is jobs."

"At least Summer Fest is an effort," Della said stubbornly. "It would bring in people and money."

"Temporarily."

"It's better than nothing. And one person acting on an idea might lead other people to action."

Sullivan considered his sister's words and the earnest look on her face. Had he been too quick to say no? Strangely, the chief going after him had not even begun to change his mind. But his sister looking at him with disapproval was something else.

It was also the wrong time to remember the tears sparkling behind Sarah McDougall's astonishing eyes.

But that's what he thought of.

"I don't like dealing with the press," he said finally. "They always manage to twist what you say. After the Algard case, if I never do another interview again it will be too soon."

Something shifted in his sister's face as he referred to the case that had finished him as a detective. Maybe even as a human being.

At any other time he might have taken advantage of her sympathy to get hold of those cookies. But it was suddenly there between them, the darkness that he had seen that separated him from this world of cookies and children's laughter that she inhabited.

They had faced the darkness, together, once before. Their parents had been murdered in a case of mistaken identity.

Della had been the one who had held what remained of their family—her and him—together.

She was the one who had kept him on the right track when it would have been so easy to let everything fall apart.

Only then, when she had made sure he finished school, had she chosen to flee her former life, the big city, the ugliness of human lives lost to violence.

And what had he done? Immersed himself in it.

"How could they twist what you had to say about saving a dog?" she asked, but her voice was softer.

"I don't present well," he said. "I come across as cold. Heartless."

"No, you don't." But she said it with a trace of doubtfulness.

"It's going to come out that I don't even like dogs."

"So you'll come across as a guy who cares only about himself. Self-centered," she concluded.

"Colossally," he agreed.

"One hundred percent pure guy."

They both laughed, her reluctantly, but still coming around. Not enough to take the cookies out of the cupboard, though. He made a little bet with himself that he'd have those cookies by the time he left here.

Wouldn't that surprise the troublemaker? That he could be charming if he chose to be?

There it was. He was thinking about *her* again. And he didn't like it one little bit. Not one.

"You should think about it," his sister persisted.

It occurred to him that if he dealt with the

press, his life would be uncomfortable for a few minutes.

If he didn't appease his sister—and his boss— his life could be miserable for a lot longer than that.

"*I* think," Della said, having given him ten seconds or so to think about it, "that you should say yes."

"For the good of the town," he said a little sourly.

"For your own good, too."

There was something about his sister that always required him to be a better man. And then there was a truth that she, and she alone, knew.

He would do anything for her.

Yet she never took advantage of that. She rarely asked him for anything.

Sullivan sighed heavily. He had a feeling he was being pushed in a direction that he did not want to go in.

At all.

CHAPTER THREE

THE phone couldn't have rung at a worse moment. Sarah was trying to shovel her latest batch of rhubarb jam into jars. How had her grandmother done this without getting jam everywhere? It was dripping down the outside of the jars, ruining the labels. She had managed to get sticky globs everywhere, including her hair!

Frisky? Sarah felt utterly exhausted.

Her phone had been ringing more than normal because of the free time on the Tally Hukas radio show yesterday, but still, she had the thought she had had every single time her phone had rung since she moved here to Kettle Bend.

She hoped it was Mike. She hoped he was phoning to beg her forgiveness. She hoped he was phoning to beg her to come back!

"I can't wait to tell him no," Sarah said, wiping goo off her hand before picking up the receiver.

Her ex-fiancé begging her forgiveness would go a long way in erasing the sourness of a heartache!

"Miss McDougall?"

It was definitely not her philandering ex-fiancé calling—Sarah would recognize that voice anywhere! She froze, licked a tiny trace of rhubarb jam off her wrist. Her heart was pounding unreasonably.

The jam seemed a little too tart.

Just like him.

"Oliver?" she said. She used his first name deliberately, hoping to aggravate him. No doubt, he was not calling voluntarily. Forced into it by the notoriety he had come into yesterday as a result of that radio show.

She enjoyed the sensation of having the upper hand.

But she also liked the way his name sounded on her lips. She had liked his name ever since she'd seen that video on the internet, and heard his name for the first time.

And this just in, fantastic footage out of Kettle Bend, Wisconsin, of Officer Oliver Sullivan...

His silence satisfied her. Then the silence was shattered by the shriek of a baby. For a stunned moment, she allowed that Oliver Sullivan might be married. There had been no ring on his finger. But lots of men did not wear rings. Especially if their line of work might make wearing them a hazard.

Sarah considered the downward swoop of her stomach with amazement. Why would she feel *bereft* if Oliver Sullivan was married?

"I'm having an emergency," he said, after a moment. "I've tried everything. I can't stop the baby from crying."

"Wh-wh-what baby?"

He had her off balance, again. He was supposed to be caving to pressure, begging her to let him do some interviews!

"My nephew, Ralf. My sister takes pity on my bachelor state—"

Bachelor state. How silly that it felt as if the light was going back on in her world!

Her world, she reminded herself sternly, was jam and Summer Fest.

"—and has me over for dinner when I'm off. But she's had a family emergency last night. Her husband was in a car accident on his way home from work. She had to leave suddenly. I don't want to call her at the hospital and tell her the baby won't stop crying. She's got enough on her plate already."

Sarah felt a faint thrill of vindication. She had just *known* this kind of man was lurking behind that remote facade he presented. The kind of man who would rescue a dog. Who would shield his sister from more anxiety.

"How is your brother-in-law?"

"Jonathon is fine. The injury is not life-threatening. It's just a complicated fracture that needs surgery. It's serious enough that she's not leaving him."

He would be like that, too, Sarah thought with a shiver. Fiercely devoted. If he ever allowed anything or anyone to get by his guard. Which seemed unlikely. Except this phone call would have seemed unlikely, too—yet here it was.

"And here I am," he said. His voice was unreasonably sexy. "Jet, get down from there! With a four-year-old nephew who is climbing the curtains and hanging off the rod. And with a baby who won't stop crying. Not knowing who to call."

Sarah was surprised to hear, beyond the sexiness, the faintest note of something else in his voice. Panic? Surely not?

"And why call me?" she asked, softly. Imagining he might say, *I saw something in your face I could not forget. You are the kind of woman a man dreams of having children with. Did you know you have a tender beauty in your eyes?*

"Your front door was open when I came by to see you the other day. I saw the framed magazines on your wall. I figured you must be some kind of expert on babies. Though, Ralf's not *today's* baby, exactly. He's eighteen months old."

"Oh." Again, not what she'd expected.

"Ah, also, I figured I had a bargaining chip with you."

"A bargaining chip?"

"You want me to do a few interviews. You have the credentials of a baby expert. Maybe we could work a trade."

It wasn't begging exactly, but it was a stunning capitulation.

Still, it was so far from her fantasy of what he might say that she burst out laughing. "I have to warn you, my knowledge of babies is pretty much theoretical." *Sadly.*

"You're *not* an expert on babies?"

"I worked for that magazine for four years. I was a writer. I interviewed new moms and wrote how-to articles." Now she felt like she was applying for a job. And one she was rather startled to find that she wanted, too!

She deliberately left out info about how many nursery remodels she had done features on, thinking he would dismiss that as frivolous. She also did not mention she knew at least a dozen remedies for diaper rash, thinking that would just make him hang up the phone! She was a hair away from having Oliver Sullivan on her team.

"Were any of those how-to articles on crying babies?" he asked. She had been right. That was desperation in his voice.

Sarah stifled a giggle at how easily a little scrap of humanity could bring a big man to his knees.

"Dozens," she said. "I've done dozens of articles on crying babies."

"He's been crying for two hours."

"Babies are very sensitive to tension," she said.

"Mine?" he asked, incredulously.

"Possibly just something in his mother's tone before she left, a change in routine, now her absence and his daddy not coming home. He knows something is amiss."

"You *are* an expert! Can you help a guy out, Sarah?"

Instead of gloating that it was his turn to beg, she focused on something else, entirely.

Not Miss McDougall. *Sarah.* Her heart feeling as if it were melting should at least serve as a warning that this was a very bad idea.

But he'd said he would do the interviews! For the good of the town, she had to suck it up.

"What do you want me to do?"

"Come over."

Suddenly it felt as if she was playing with fire. She was *way* too happy to be talking to him, and it wasn't just because their arrangement was going to be good for the town, either.

Don't go over there, she warned herself. She could make suggestions over the phone. She could protect herself from whatever dumb thing her heart was doing right now.

Beating in double time.

Sarah caught a glimpse of herself in the mirror over the kitchen sink. She was blushing crazily, like a preteen girl getting her first call from a boy. She had her new life to think about. She had the new *her* to think about—independent, not susceptible to the painful foibles of the human heart.

She, Sarah McDougall, had learned her lessons!

She heard a crash and a howl. "What was that?"

"The living room curtains just came down. My nephew Jet was attached to them."

"I'll be right there."

"Really?"

"Really."

He gave her the address.

"Bring some of that jam," he suggested, "Crabbies, right? The one your grandmother said relieved crankiness. If ever a guy needed it, it's this one."

"You or the baby?"

"Both," he said ruefully.

Sarah knew she should not be so flattered that he seemed to remember every single thing she had said to him.

"Could you hurry?"

If she didn't hurry she would have an opportunity to make a better second impression on Oliver Sullivan. She could do her hair and her makeup. She could throw on something flirty and fabulous. But the baby in the background, his little voice hoarse, hiccupping his distress, did seem to give the situation a sense of urgency.

Plus, she did not want to give in to that urge to make Sullivan find her attractive. The situation she was heading into was dangerous enough without the complication of attraction between them.

Five minutes later, she shut her door, trying very hard not to acknowledge how happy she was to be escaping from her sticky jam jars.

Moments later, Sarah arrived at the door of a charming little bungalow that was very much like hers, at least on the outside.

When Sullivan came to the door, she realized trying to halt that particular complication—

attraction—would be like trying to hold back the tide.

The man was glorious.

A few days ago, he had been all icy composure. Today, the man who came to the door was every bit as compelling as the one she had seen in the video with the puppy.

His dark chocolate hair was mussed. His sculpted face was shadowed with unshaven whiskers. The remoteness of his dark eyes was layered with exhaustion, a compelling kind of vulnerability. His shirt had damp tear blotches on it.

And in his arms was a baby.

A distraught baby, to be sure, but even so, there was something breathtaking about the contrast between such a strong man, and the baby in his arms. His muscled arm curved around the baby's behind, holding him firmly into the broadness of his chest.

For all that he was exhausted, there was something in Sullivan's stance that said it all. This baby, fragile, vulnerable, needy, was safe with him. It would come to no harm on his watch.

A little boy squeezed between Sullivan's legs and the screen door, and pushed on it. When it gave way, he gave a little whoop of freedom, which was short-lived when his uncle freed a hand, snatched his collar and pulled him back in the house. He would come to no harm on his uncle's watch, either.

The little boy, like a wind-up toy that had hit an obstacle, changed direction and darted off down a hallway.

"Come in," he invited over the howling of the baby and the screeching of his other nephew echoing from deep within the house.

She had known coming here was entering a danger zone like none she had ever known. Seeing Oliver Sullivan standing there, with that baby in his arms, confirmed it.

He still looked every inch a warrior, strong, *ready*, formidable.

But she suspected his exhaustion, his sudden

immersion into a battle of a totally different sort, one he was obviously ill-prepared to deal with, had him as close to surrender as she would ever find him.

Surrender to what? she asked herself. *Being vulnerable. Attraction. Being human.*

Run, she told herself.

But running would look foolish and she didn't want to look foolish to him. Some despicably traitorous part of her wanted to look as attractive to him as he did to her.

Perhaps she could look at this as a test of her resolve. This was a test of how deeply committed she was to a life of giving her heart only to something inanimate, that could not hurt her, like a town.

Taking a deep breath, Sarah stepped in the open door. The air had a scorched smell to it.

As if the devil had been hard at work, creating a perfect potion to tempt her away from the life she had chosen for herself.

The baby was part of that potion, adorable,

radiating sweetness despite the lustiness of his howls. He twisted his head and regarded her solemnly. His face was blotchy from crying. His voice was a croak of indignation.

"Hello, sweetie," she said softly.

The baby stopped, mid caterwaul, and regarded her with both suspicion and hope.

"Mama," he whispered.

"I know, baby. You miss your Mommy, don't you?"

A thumb went into a mouth and he slurped thoughtfully, nodded, squeezed out a few additional tears, then reached out both pudgy arms for her.

Sullivan said a word under his breath that you weren't supposed to say around babies and passed the child to her.

Sarah slid her bag off her shoulder onto the floor, then took the surprising weight of the baby in her arms. As if seeing Sullivan holding the baby hadn't been bad enough, experiencing the baby's warm, cuddly body pressed against her breast increased the squishy feeling inside of her.

"His name is Ralf," Sullivan said, his voice low, unintentionally sensual, the voice of a man afraid to speak in fear of getting the baby going again.

"Hello, Ralf, I'm Sarah."

"Want Mama." Sarah stepped over an overturned tricycle into a living room that had been ransacked. The curtain bar was up on one side and ripped down on the other. Books had been pulled off the shelves and scattered. A diaper sack had fallen over and was spilling its contents onto the floor. She cleared a jumble of toys off the couch and sank down on it, pressing the baby into her shoulder.

"Of course you want your mama," she said soothingly. "She'll be home as soon as she can. Does he still take a bottle?" she asked Sullivan.

"A bottle of what?" he asked, baffled.

"Rye whiskey," she teased with a shake of her

head. "Go check the fridge and see if there are any baby bottles in there."

"There are!" he called, a moment later, with relief. "I've just been feeding him that baby gruel stuff. I didn't know he still took a bottle."

"Okay, heat it up in the microwave for a few seconds and bring it here."

He galloped in with the bottle.

"Did you test it to make sure it's not too hot?"

Sullivan looked at her as if her request was untenable. He glanced at the bottle, grimaced, then lifted it, a soldier prepared to do what needed to be done.

"No!" she said, just in time. "You test it on your wrist!"

"Oh." With relief, he shook a few drops of the milk in the bottle onto his wrist. His wrist was large, and square and strong, making her ultra-aware of the sizzling masculine appeal of him.

He handed her the bottle a little sheepishly. "See? An expert. I knew you'd know what to do."

Shaking her head, she took the bottle from him,

nestled Ralf in the crook of her arm and put the bottle to his lips.

With an aggrieved look at his uncle and a sigh, he nestled more deeply into her, wrapped his lips against the bottle and began to make the cutest little *slurp-slurp* sound. The tiny slurping sounds grew farther and farther apart.

Within seconds the baby was asleep.

Sullivan was staring at her as if she had parted the sea.

"I can't believe that."

"He was exhausted, ready to go no matter what."

"I owe you big-time."

"Yes, you do."

His gratitude was colossally short-lived. He folded his arms over his stained chest and rocked back on his heels. "Three interviews. No parade marshal."

"I see I should have driven my bargain while he was screaming," she said ruefully. But inside she savored her victory. He was going to do it!

He was going to help her save Kettle Bend by making it the best Summer Fest the town had ever had.

"I have to warn you, I'm not good at interviews. I have a talent for saying exactly the wrong thing," he said ruefully.

"Luckily for you, in my past life, I've interviewed tons of people. I know the kind of questions they'll ask you. Why don't I come up with a list, and we can do a practice run?"

What did that have to do with getting away from this man as quickly as possible?

The little boy, Jet, came back in, tucked himself behind his uncle's leg and peered out at her.

"I'm Sarah," she said.

"I'm hungry."

"Hello, hungry."

"Sullivan burned supper."

"He doesn't call you Uncle Oliver?" Sarah asked, surprised.

"I told you no one calls me Oliver."

"Who's Oliver?" Jet asked with a scowl, and

then repeated, a little more stridently, "I'm hungry!"

"What's your favorite thing to eat?" she asked him.

"Mac and cheese. He burned it."

"How about your second favorite thing?" A picture of her cooking dinner for them crowded her mind. It occurred to her it was way too cozy. If attraction could be complicated, what would sharing such a domestic scene be?

She pictured washing dishes with Sullivan and then felt annoyed with herself. Is this what her life had become that she could find washing dishes with a man romantic?

Of course, she thought, as she slid the man in question a look, there wasn't much she could do with him that wouldn't feel romantic.

Which was a big problem.

"My second favorite food is Hombre hamburgers!" Jet crowed.

Sarah felt a twinge of regret that was far larger than her twinge of relief. Hombre's was a favorite

Kettle Bend eatery just a few blocks away. It was a plan for supper that didn't need to include her.

"That sounds like a perfect solution for supper," Sarah said brightly to Sullivan. "You can pop the baby in the stroller, and he'll sleep all the way there."

She stood, a bit clumsily with the baby in arms. "It looks like your emergency is over, Oliver."

"Who's Oliver?" Jet demanded again.

She held out the sleeping baby. Sullivan took him, reluctantly.

"Don't go," he pleaded. "He's going to wake up sometime."

"Well, I can't stay all night."

The blush moved up her cheeks like fire, as if she had propositioned him. Or he her.

He had the audacity to look amused by it.

"No, but walk down to Hombre's with us. I'll buy you a hamburger. It's the least I can do," he wheedled.

Oh, boy. Sitting across the table from him in a restaurant would be worse than doing dishes with him. A fantasy of a happy family crowded her mind.

Of course, if her own family was anything to go by, that's exactly what happy families were. A fantasy.

One she had believed in, despite her upbringing. Or maybe because of it. One that had made her so needy for love that she had fallen for the wrong person.

She could feel that neediness in her still, and knew that was the demon she needed to fight.

"The least you can do is for me is four interviews," she said.

"Three," he replied.

"Four, if I join you at Hombre's."

What was she doing? She couldn't play at happy families with this man. She couldn't. What had made her say that, when she already knew she had to get herself out that door and away from him? Her new life was wavering in front of her like a distant mirage on a scorching desert day.

The look of amusement around his eyes deepened.

It made him more attractive than ever, even though he didn't smile. Good grief, she hoped he wouldn't smile. She'd be lost.

"I have to say that's the first time anyone has ever made me bargain with them to go on a date."

She stared at him. "A date?" she squeaked, and then forced herself to regain her composure. He was just that type of man. No, he would not have to bargain with women to go on dates with him. They would throw themselves at his feet for the opportunity.

She had been weak like that, once, but she was no more.

"I don't do dates," she said crisply.

She saw way too much register in his eyes, as if she had laid out every pathetic detail of her broken engagement to him.

"I didn't mean a *date* date." Was his tone almost gentle? Somehow, from the moment she'd first seen him risk his life for the dog, she had known there was a gentle side to him. But to see it in his eyes now and know it was pity? She hated that!

Of course he hadn't asked her on a *date*. She could feel herself squirm at the very assumption she'd made.

"Four interviews if you come to Hombre's. Not on a date. How would a date be possible with these munchkins watching our every move?" he teased.

Dumb to wonder what he would consider a date, then. Obviously it would involve something that he wouldn't want his nephews to see!

Her eyes moved involuntarily to his lips. Would he kiss on the first date? Even allowing herself to ponder the question seemed weak and juvenile. He was obviously a mature man, somewhat hardened and certainly cynical. Possibly he would expect quite a bit more than a kiss on a first date.

She had to stop this, right now. The conjecture was making her feel as if she was burning up, coming down with a fever.

He could take his nephews to Hombre's by himself.

But he might need me, a voice inside her quibbled.

No, that wasn't the truth at all. The truth was, Sarah wanted to spend more time with him.

She tried to tell herself it was because anything would be better than going back to that jam. But she knew it was more, something leaping in the air between them, that baby creating moments of vulnerability in her that were bringing barriers down that needed to be up!

Sullivan was looking at her so intently she thought she would melt.

"Uh, maybe you'd want to do something with your hair," he said after a moment. "I think it has something in it." He reached over and touched it.

His touch was so brief. But it made her aware of a very real danger of the awareness that sizzled in the air between them.

Or maybe not. Mortified, she watched as he

looked at the blob on his finger, and then sniffed it. Then he put it to his lips and tasted.

And smiled.

That smile was just as devastating as Sarah had known it would be.

She felt weak from how it changed him, the guarded look swept from his face, revealing a hint of the light that he kept well hidden inside himself.

"It's jam," he said. "Crabbies?"

"No. Crabbies is made from crab apples. This is rhubarb. My grandmother called it Spring Fling." She blushed again when she said it, as if she had said something off-color and provocative.

"So, if Crabbies can cure crankiness, what can a Spring Fling do?" he asked and raised a wicked eyebrow at her.

What could a spring fling do? Somehow Sarah didn't want to tell him abut the promised friskiness of the jam. Or of its promised properties to erase the sourness of a heartache and herald in new hope.

"It's just jam," she said, "it can't *do* anything."

"Not a bad hair pomade, though," he said seriously.

She laughed, reluctantly, and he laughed, too. If his smile had been devastating to her carefully laid plans for her new life, his laughter was downright dangerous.

It revealed something so *real* about him. It intrigued her. It made her wonder why he was so guarded, so closed off, so deliberately unapproachable.

It made her want to rescue him from himself. It occurred to her it was the first time since her breakup that she had allowed herself to feel curious about a man.

It seemed new hope had crept into her life whether she wanted it or not.

And she did want it.

Just not from this source! People—particularly *men*—were too unpredictable. Mike had already taught her that.

Even before Mike, her father had ripped apart her own family. She would forget the lessons she had learned from the men in her life at her own peril.

Hadn't Michael Talbot *seemed* totally decent? Reliable? Even a touch staid? Exactly the kind of man one could count on building a life with?

Hadn't her father seemed like that, too? A partner in a law firm, the epitome of success by any standard?

But this man who stood before her was nothing like Mike. And nothing like her father, either. Oliver Sullivan seemed full of contradictions and dark mysteries. Something in him was deeply wounded.

It would be a mistake to think you could fix something like that without getting hurt yourself.

"I can't possibly take the children to Hombre's with you," she said quickly before she could change her mind. "Not possibly. Three interviews will be just fine. More than enough. I'll call you with the details when I've set it up."

She turned and bolted from the house, aware of his curious eyes on her, but not daring to look back.

CHAPTER FOUR

So, SHE didn't date, Sullivan thought, watching Sarah scurry down his sister's sidewalk and get in her car. She drove away with haste, a quick shoulder check, and a spin of tires.

That whole incident had been very telling for a man who read people with such stripping accuracy.

Sarah McDougall didn't date.

She was as cute as a button, refreshingly natural, obviously single and in the prime of her life. She probably had guys falling at her feet. And she didn't date?

Plus, she was devoting herself to what could very well be a lost cause, the rebirth of Kettle Bend through its Summer Fest. But at least, he saw with clarity, it was a cause that couldn't hurt her.

Heartbreak, he told himself. She'd suffered a heartbreak.

And from the way she looked holding that baby? Like a Madonna, completely serene, completely fulfilled. Her heartbreak hadn't done one little thing to cure her of what she really wanted. Her longings had been written in the tender expression on her face, in the little smile, in her unconscious sigh as that baby had settled against her.

Sarah McDougall wanted a family. Babies. Security.

She'd been wise to leave.

And he'd been wise to let her. Their life goals were at cross purposes. His was to do his job and do it well. His kind of work did not lend itself to the kind of cozy life she craved. It required a hard man who was prepared to do hard things.

People, including her, wanted to believe something else because of the video of him rescuing the puppy. But Sullivan knew himself—and his limitations—extremely well.

Sarah's life goal—no matter what she had convinced herself—had been written all over her when she'd had that baby pressed to her breast.

The other thing he could tell about her was that she was one of those naive people who believed she could use the force of her will to mold a happy world. Her devotion to Summer Fest was proof of that.

He was pretty sure he could kill her illusions in about ten minutes. Not deliberately. It was just the dark cynicism he'd developed for dealing with a tough, cold, hard world. If her illusions made her happy, even if they were hopelessly naive, he should just leave her alone with them.

Their lives would tangle once more because he'd agreed to do the interviews. Then he would put her behind him. Along with this strange yearning he felt every time he saw her.

Rest.

"I don't need a rest," he said out loud, annoyed. The baby woke up with a sputter and Jet raced by, his mother's lipstick streaked across his face like war paint.

"Except from that."

The next day, Sarah called him on his cell phone. He was at work, but it was an exceptionally quiet morning, even for Kettle Bend. It would have been a good morning to start cleaning cars, but somehow he wasn't. So far, some foolish sense of pride had prevented him from telling the chief he'd agreed to do the interviews, after all.

Sullivan registered, a little uneasily, that he felt happy to hear her voice.

"How's your brother-in-law?"

She would ask that first, a tenderness in her, an ability to care and to love deeply. Busy making her own happy world, whether she would admit to it or not.

Which meant he had to put a red warning flag beside her in his mind. Oh, wait, he'd already done that! So he shouldn't be all that happy to hear from her. But he could not deny that he was.

He tried to tell himself that between Sarah and cleaning cars, she was the clear winner. It didn't *mean* anything.

"The surgery went well. No complications. He'll be in the hospital a little longer, but my sister got home late last night."

Silence. He could tell that she wanted to ask him how the baby had been, and if they'd gone for their supper at Hombre's after all.

But she didn't. Evidently all her warning flags were waving, too.

Which was a good thing. A very good thing.

He could hear her trying to keep the distance in her voice when she asked if they could meet. She had set up the interviews and, as promised, would run a few potential questions by him.

That was perfect. She was all business. It would be good to get it over with and put his very short Sarah McDougall chapter behind him.

"Do you want me to come by your place?" he asked.

"Uh, no."

He felt relieved. There was something about her place, the coziness of those yellow sofas facing each other over drooping flowers that would not lend itself to the barriers he felt were essential to keep up between them.

"I'm in a jam. Literally," Sarah said.

He heard something in her voice that gave him pause. "You don't really like making jam, do you?" he asked quietly.

He could have kicked himself. A question like that was personal! It had nothing to do with keeping barriers up. It was as if he'd said to her, *You're not fulfilled. How come? What's up? What's getting in the way of your happy fantasy?*

The question, he told himself firmly, was what was up with him, not her!

Luckily, his question actually seemed to succeed at putting a barrier up, not taking one down.

"What would make you say that?" she asked defensively. "I happen to *love* my grandmother's business. I *love* making jam."

Leave it.

But he didn't. His *uh-huh* was loaded with disbelief.

"I do!"

A woman, if there ever was one, who was made to say *I do.* To believe in forever after.

Talking about jam, he reminded himself firmly, furious that his mind had gone there.

He could tell she was fuming. Well, it wasn't his fault that he was pretty good at reading most people, and really good at reading her in particular. Besides, fuming was good. Barriers up!

"So, where do you want to meet?" he asked.

Her voice was cool. "How about Winston's Church Hill Coffee Shoppe? What's your schedule like? Could you do it in half an hour?"

Winston's was always loud. And crowded. Very public. A good choice. He wished she had picked Grady's, which had booths and better coffee.

"Winston's would be the best," she said, as if she had read his mind. "It'll be crowded. It'll go through town like wildfire that you met me there. It might undo some of the damage to your popularity the radio show caused."

Yeah, Winston's was the town rumor mill, not that Sullivan gave a fig about popularity.

He was working. He was in uniform. That might be a good thing. There was nothing like a uniform to keep his distance from people.

She was already there when he walked into the coffee shop, bent over some papers, her tongue caught between her teeth in concentration.

He hesitated for a moment, studying her.

Sarah didn't look like she had looked yesterday at his sister's, or the way she had looked in her garden, either.

She was wearing a sundress the color of her sofa, summer-afternoon yellow. It hugged the slenderness of her curves, showed off skin already faintly sun-kissed, brought his eye to a little gold heart that winked at the vulnerable hollow of her throat.

She'd done something to her hair, too. The curls had been tamed, straightened, and her hair hung in a glossy wave to the swell of shoulders that were naked save for the thin strap of the dress.

When she glanced up, he saw that she had put on makeup and that her eyes looked dazzling. But not as dazzling as her freshly glossed lips.

It worried him that all this might be for him.

But as soon as he joined her, he saw this was her barrier, as much as his uniform was his.

She was here as a professional woman.

Sarah wore that role with an ease and comfort that was very telling.

Though he'd decided he wasn't going to try and tell her anything anymore. She was a little too touchy. It was none of his business that she was trying to run from the very things that gave her the most satisfaction.

Babies.

Her career.

There was no reason the two things could not coexist, he thought.

Not that it was any of his concern.

She got down to business right away.

"You'll be happy to know we're just going to do one interview."

We're.

"I've arranged for you to do one interview, which will be taped with the local television station. The news anchor, Bradley Moore, will do it, and then they'll send it to their national affiliates."

He was impressed. She was a professional. "Perfect."

"I think you should wear your uniform." Her eyes drifted over him, and despite his determination to untangle their lives after this task was completed, he was more than a little pleased by what he saw.

She liked a man in uniform.

"So, just pretend I'm the person interviewing you."

A waitress came by and filled his coffee cup without asking him.

"So, Officer Sullivan," Sarah said, putting on

her interviewer hat, "what did you do before you came to Kettle Bend?"

"I was a homicide detective in Detroit."

"Couldn't you elaborate?" she prodded him.

"No, I couldn't."

She dropped the interviewer hat. "But it's a perfect opportunity to introduce the charms of Kettle Bend to the conversation. You could say that you tired of the coldly impersonal life in the big city and chose the warmth and friendliness of Kettle Bend instead."

"To tell you the truth I had no objection to the coldly impersonal life in Detroit. I could go get my groceries without someone telling me there was a car illegally parked on their block. Or worse, asking me about that blasted dog," he said caustically.

"You can't call him *that blasted dog*," she said, horrified. "Why did you move here if you liked your coldly impersonal life so much?"

He shocked himself by saying, "I burned out," and then, irritated at himself for saying it, and annoyed at the warmly curious look in her expression, he changed the subject.

"I don't like dogs," he said. It might as well come out. It might as well come out as a way of keeping her at bay. He took a sip of his coffee and watched her closely over the lip of the mug to see what her response to that would be.

"You can't say you don't like dogs!" she said. "What kind of person doesn't like dogs?"

Perfect. The kind of person little Sarah McDougall should be very cautious of.

"I'm not the warm and fuzzy type," he warned her. "And that does not translate well in interviews. I'm not going to lie about liking dogs. I'm not going to lie about anything."

"I'm not asking you to lie!" she protested.

"That's good."

"Okay," she said, determined, looking at her notes. "So, you don't like dogs. I'm sure you could gloss over that without *lying*. Something like, *there are dog people and cat people. I'm a cat person*. Maybe that would make your leap into the river seem even more heroic."

"I'm getting a headache," he said. "And I don't like cats, either."

"Horses?" she said, hopefully.

"I'm not an animal person."

"Not an animal person," she repeated, faintly distressed.

"There are animal people and not animal people. I'm in the 'not' category."

"Why wouldn't you like animals?" she asked.

Don't tell her the truth. But he couldn't help himself. "I don't like neediness. I don't want anything relying on me. I don't want to become attached to anything." He didn't have to elaborate. In fact, he ordered himself not to elaborate. Then… "I don't want to love anything."

They both sat there in shocked silence.

"But why?" she finally ventured.

Don't say it. She doesn't have to know. There is no reason for her to know.

"My parents were killed when I was seventeen." He *hated* himself for saying it. Why was he admitting all this stuff to her? It felt as if she were pulling his insides out of him without really trying, just looking at him with those warm, understanding eyes.

Sullivan pulled back into damage-control mode as quickly as he could. "That had better not come out in the interview. I don't want any sympathy. From anyone."

Her mouth had opened as if she was going to say something sympathetic. She correctly interpreted his glare, and her mouth closed slowly. But she couldn't do anything about her eyes.

They had softened to a shade of gold that reminded him of the setting sun, gentle, caressing, not simply sympathetic, somehow. Sharing his pain with him.

He shrugged uncomfortably. "Don't worry. I'm not going to say in public that I don't like dogs because I don't want to get attached to anything. I'm not even sure why I said it to you."

He was already very sorry he had.

He glanced at his watch, a hint for her to move on, and was unreasonably grateful when she did.

"So what are you going to say when or if you're asked why you jumped in the river to save the dog?" she asked curiously.

"Momentary insanity?" He looked at her face, and sighed. "I'll say I thought it probably belonged to the kid I'd seen riding his bike across the bridge earlier, and that I didn't want him to lose his dog."

"Oh," she said, pleased, "that's nice."

Nice. She wasn't getting it. Oliver Sullivan was not *nice*.

"As it turned out," he said gruffly, "the puppy didn't belong to him. They still haven't found the owner. The dog's going up for adoption next week if he isn't claimed."

"That would be good to mention. That would bring a lot of attention to Kettle Bend."

"Believe me, it already has. The police station had a call from Germany last week asking about the dog."

"If you can say that, that would be wonderful! People in Germany interested in Kettle Bend! An international angle!"

"I'll try to work it in," he said. Her enthusiasm should have been annoying. Instead, it seemed as cute as her sunshine-yellow dress. She seemed to have an absolute gift for making his mind go places it did not want to go, breaking down barriers that he had thought were high and fortified.

"Now," she tapped her pencil against her lips, "how could you work in Summer Fest?"

He groaned, and not entirely because of the mention of Summer Fest. She had drawn his attention to her lips, which were full and plump.

Kissable.

"I don't understand your cynicism about it," she said, pursing those delicious lips now.

"I'm cynical about everything." He covered his fascination with her lips by taking a swig of his coffee.

"No, you're not."

Oh, Sarah, do yourself a favor and do not be-lieve the best in me.

"Look," he said, "I think it's naive to believe a little festival can do much for a town. I don't understand exactly what you think it's going to do for Kettle Bend."

"It's going to bring back the summer visitors. It's going to revitalize things. It's going to bring in some much-needed money. It's going to put us on the map again, as a destination. All those people who come here are going to realize what a great place this would be to come live."

Let her have her illusions, Sullivan ordered himself. But he didn't. In fact, he suddenly felt as if he was done with illusions. Like the one that he would ever taste those delectable lips.

His cynicism, his dark history, could put out that light that radiated off of her in about three seconds.

"You know, Sarah, I haven't been here long, but this town is suffering because some of its major employers are gone. The factories are shut down.

How can it be a great place to live if there are no jobs here? What Kettle Bend really needs is jobs. Real jobs. Permanent jobs."

"Your sister and her family moved here," she said defensively.

"Jonathon has to commute to Madison. He keeps an apartment close to work for the days he's too tired to drive home. He makes a lot of sacrifices so my sister can have her fantasy of small-town life. I think his accident probably resulted from the fatigue of the constant commuting."

"Did you tell your sister that?" she asked, clearly horrified.

"I did." Unfortunately. So he was still off the cookie list, even though he had told his sister he would do the interviews arranged by Sarah, after all.

"You shouldn't have said that to your sister."

"No practice runs about what to say in real life," he said, putting unnecessary emphasis on *real life*.

She flinched. He covered his remorse by taking a sip of coffee.

"Summer Fest is going to help Kettle Bend," she said stubbornly.

"I've done a bit of checking. It was cancelled because there was no way of measuring whether the output of money could be justified by a temporary influx of visitors."

"I'm being very careful with the budget I've been given. I'm supplementing it with several fundraisers," she said.

"I know. My sister is donating *my* cookies to the bake sale." The very thought soured him. Well, that and the fact Sarah McDougall, with her kind eyes and her sunshiny dress, had ferreted information out of him that he was in no way ready to divulge.

"You know what I think?" He knew he was about to be a little nasty.

He also knew this was more about his lapse—his confiding in her—than it was about Summer Fest. He had to get his walls back up before she crashed right through them and found herself in a land where she didn't want to be.

He needed her to know, beyond a shadow of a doubt, he didn't want or need her sympathy. He wanted to drive what remained of that gentle look out of her eyes.

The kind of look that could make a hard man soft.

A strong man weak.

The kind of look that made a man who had lost faith in any kind of goodness feel just a smidgen of doubt about his own solitary stance.

"What do you think?" But she asked tentatively, something in him making her wary. As well it should.

"You think immersing yourself in Summer Fest is going to help you get over your heartbreak," he said.

She stiffened. He was relieved to see that look—as if her heart was big enough to hold all her own troubles and his too—evaporating from her eyes.

"What heartbreak?" she said warily.

"A girl like you doesn't come to a town like this unless you're trying to outrun something."

"That's not true!" she sputtered.

He looked at her coolly. Maybe it was because she'd somehow made him blurt out his own truth that he needed to show her he could see hers. No, it wasn't that complicated.

He was trying to drive her away.

Before he became *attached*.

"You know, Summer Fest can't make you feel the way you felt when you came here as a kid. No matter how successful it is."

"How do you know what I felt as a kid?" she asked in a shrill whisper.

He snorted. "You felt as if your every dream could come true. You were full of hope and romantic illusions."

She stared at him, two little twin spots of anger growing bright on her cheeks. Then she got up abruptly. She tossed her neatly printed sheet of questions at him.

"Here. You look at these questions yourself. I'm sure you can come up with some answers that won't manage to offend every single person who watches you on television."

He'd made her very angry. He'd hurt her. In the long run that was only a good thing.

Because there was something about her that made a guy want to say way too much, reveal way too much.

There was something about her that made a man wonder what his life could have been like if he had been dealt a different deck, or chosen a different road.

He watched her through the window, walking away from the coffee shop, her hips swishing with anger, the yellow dress swirling around her slender legs.

He picked up the papers she had tossed down, pulled on his cap and pulled the brim low over his eyes.

His uniform, his job, had always been a shield

that protected him. How was it she had broken right through it, without half trying?

And why was it, that even though he had succeeded in driving her off, she had succeeded in piquing his curiosity, too? He had uncovered some truth about her, but it felt like it wasn't enough.

As a former detective he had all kinds of ways of finding things out about people without their ever knowing he had….

Sarah was furious. "Of all the smug, bigheaded, supercilious, self-important jerks," she muttered to herself, walking fast away from the café, her head high. "How dare he?"

It had really started with the phone call.

You don't really like making jam, do you?

Then it had just gone all downhill from there.

You think immersing yourself in Summer Fest is going to help you get over your heartbreak.

It was humiliating that somehow he knew that she'd had a heartbreak, as if she were some pathetic cat lady whose life tragedies were apparent to all! It was particularly nasty that he'd had the bad manners to call her on it.

And telling her that she was using Summer Fest to try and recapture the dreams of her youth was mean.

Oliver Sullivan was just plain *mean*.

She hoped he blew the interviews. She hoped the whole world hated him as much as she did! At this moment, she was too angry to care if it damaged Summer Fest!

She stomped into her house, and slammed the door extra hard when the smell of cooked rhubarb hit her.

She went and ripped off the gorgeous little sundress that she had always loved, and put on old clothes that wouldn't be ruined by making jam all afternoon. She had loved putting on that dress again!

Then suddenly it hit her.

The enormity of the thought made her sink down on her bed.

With a meow of pure contentment her cat, Sushi, found her lap and settled on it.

He'd done it on purpose. Oliver Sullivan had made her mad on purpose.

And he'd done it because he'd given something to her. He had trusted her with parts of himself. He had told her things he was not accustomed to revealing. He'd come out from behind his barriers for a little while.

And then he had gone into full retreat!

He'd succeeded, though. She bet he was feeling mighty pleased with himself right now because he'd managed to drive her away.

Sitting there on her bed she contemplated the loneliness of Sullivan's world. At least she had her cat. At least she wasn't so damaged she couldn't even get attached to an animal.

And she was making a ton of friends here in her adopted town. She adored her neighbors, she was developing friendships with many of the volunteers on the Summer Fest committees.

He had chosen a world and a job that could isolate him.

"I'm going in after him," she said out loud, shocking herself. Where had that come from?

She contemplated the absolute insanity of it, and then laughed out loud. She didn't care if it felt insane.

Sarah felt alive. Something she had not felt since Mike had driven the spike of betrayal right through her heart.

It was something she had not felt when she moved to her grandmother's house. She had certainly not felt it stirring endless pots of jam. And Summer Fest had not made her feel like this, either.

She felt *needed.*

She felt like she could put her petty need to protect herself on hold.

She felt that she had a mission, a man to save from himself, to rescue. He had shown her that brief glimpse of himself for a reason. She was not going to turn her back on him. She was not going to leave him in that dark, lonely place.

And she knew exactly how she was going to do it, too.

"I'm going to use the puppy."

Sushi gave a shrill meow of pure betrayal and jumped off her lap.

Sarah's confidence had dwindled somewhat by the time she arrived at Sullivan's house, unannounced. Obviously, if she called him to warn him of her arrival with the dog, he would just say no.

Of course, there was plenty of potential for him to just say no, regardless.

She was also beginning to understand why Sullivan did not like dogs. Sarah's experience with dogs was very limited. The charm of the adorable cuteness of the puppy—soulful eyes, huge paws, curly black hair—wore off in about five seconds.

The puppy was rambunctious. His greeting this morning when he had been let out of his kennel in his temporary quarters at the vet's office had been way too enthusiastic.

He was gigantic, the vet said, probably some Newfoundland or Bouvier blood—and possibly a combination of both—making him so large even though he was only about four months old.

He had nearly knocked Sarah off her feet with his joy in seeing her. Her yoga pants—picked because they were both flattering and appropriate for an outing with a dog—now had a large snag running from thigh to calf.

The puppy flung himself against the leash, nearly pulling her shoulder out of the socket. Once in her car, he had found a box of tissue in the backseat and shredded it entirely on the short drive to Sullivan's house.

Sullivan had insinuated she didn't have a clue about real life.

The puppy seemed determined to prove him correct. *Real* puppies were not fun like fantasy puppies.

So, Sarah was already questioning the wisdom

of the idea that had seemed so perfect in the sanctuary of her bedroom.

The puppy was reminding her that reality and fantasy were often on a collision course.

Still, she was here now, and there was no turning back. So, ignoring the beating of her heart, unwrapping the leash from around her legs for at least the twentieth time, she went up the stairs.

Sullivan's house was not like her house. And not like his sister's. There were no flowers, there was no swing on the porch.

Everything was in order, and it was immaculate, but there was nothing welcoming about his house. There were no planters, no rugs, no porch furniture, no screen door in front of the storm door.

Because he doesn't welcome anybody, she reminded herself. He pushes away. That's why she was here.

With a renewed sense of mission, she took a deep breath, ordered the dog to sit, and was ignored, and then rang Sullivan's doorbell.

He didn't answer, and she rang it again.

Just when she thought the whole idea was a bust—he wasn't home, despite her careful and clever ferreting out of his schedule—she heard a noise inside the house. He was in there. He'd probably peered out the window, seen it was her and decided not to answer his door.

She rang the bell again. And again. Then gave the door a frustrated kick. As a result, she nearly fell inside when his door was suddenly flung open.

Oliver Sullivan stood in front of her, wearing only a towel, his naked chest beaded with water, his dark hair plastered against his head like melted chocolate.

Sarah gulped as his eyes swept her, coolly, took in the dog, and then he planted his legs far apart and folded his muscled arms across the masculine magnificence of his deep, deep chest.

The whiteness of the towel, riding low and knotted at his hip, made his skin seem golden and sensuous. Steam was rising off his heated body.

That first day he had appeared in her garden, she had foolishly imagined how his skin would smell fresh out of the shower.

But again, she could see fantasy and reality were on a collision course.

Because his scent was better than anything she could have ever, ever imagined. It was heady, masculine, crisp, clean. His scent tickled her nostrils like bubbles from freshly uncorked champagne.

It occurred to her she had been very, very wrong to come here. Her reasoning had been flawed.

Because Sarah had never seen a man less in need of rescuing than this one.

He was totally self-reliant, totally strong, totally sure of himself.

And he was nearly naked.

Which made her the exact opposite of all those things! She dropped her eyes, which didn't help one little bit. Staring at the perfect cut of his water-slicked naked legs, she felt totally weak and unsure of herself.

She forced herself to look back at his face. His gaze was unyielding. She opened her mouth, and not a single sound came out.

The puppy, however, was not paralyzed. With an ecstatic yelp of recognition, it yanked free of the leash, and hurled itself at Sullivan. It jumped up on its back legs, scrabbled at his naked chest with his front paws, whining, begging for affection and attention.

One of those frantically waving paws clawed down the washboard of perfect abs and caught in the towel.

Before Sarah's horrified eyes, the dog yanked his paw free of where it had become entangled in the towel. That scrap of white terry cloth was ripped from Sullivan's waist and floated to the ground.

CHAPTER FIVE

SARAH kept her eyes glued on the puddle of white towel on the porch floor.

Sullivan said three words in a row, universal expressions of extreme masculine displeasure. Then, thankfully, his feet backed out of her line of vision. It was really the wrong time to think he had very sexy feet!

The dog's feet also left her line of vision, Sullivan using him as some sort of shield as he backed into his house.

The front door slammed closed.

Sarah dared to lift her eyes. She wanted to bolt off the porch and go home, crawl into bed and pull the covers over her head.

Rescue Oliver Sullivan? Was she crazy? She needed to get out of here before she was faced with the full repercussions of her impulsiveness!

But there was the little question of the dog she had brought. She was going to have to face the music. Tempting as it was, she couldn't just dump the dog here—at the mercy of a man who had admitted he didn't like dogs—and run home.

With nothing to sit on, she settled on the steps, chin in hands, trying to think of anything but that startling moment when the towel had fallen.

The door swished open a few minutes later, and Sarah scrambled to her feet and turned to face him. He had put on a pair of jeans, but his chest was still bare. And so were his sexy feet.

Wordlessly, he passed her the dog's leash, folded his arms over his chest and raised an eyebrow at her.

She didn't know what had happened in the house, but Sullivan had obviously proved himself the dominant member of the pack. The dog was subdued. It sat quietly, eyes glued adoringly on him.

"What do you want?"

Was there an unfortunate emphasis on *you* as

if he would have rather seen anyone else on his door—vacuum cleaner salesman, Girl Scouts with cookies, old women with religious tracts?

"Um," Sarah said, tucking a loose strand of hair behind her ear, and making a pattern on his porch with her sneaker, "the TV station asked if you could bring the dog to your interview."

"I must have missed the memo where you scheduled the interview," he said, not making this easy for her.

"It's actually scheduled for tomorrow, at 6:00 p.m. but given how you feel about dogs, I thought maybe you and the dog should bond a little first."

"Bond," he said flatly.

"I didn't want it to be obvious to the viewers during the interview that you didn't like dogs."

"Bond," he repeated. "With a dog."

"Would you?" she asked hopefully. She dared glance up at him. She was encouraged to see he had not just gone back into his house and slammed the door. "There's a dog park in Westside. I thought maybe you could go and throw a stick for him. Just so that you look like buddies for the interview."

"Look like buddies," he said, his voice still flat, his arms crossed, his body language completely uninviting, "with a dog."

She nodded, but nothing in the stern lines of his face gave her any reason to hope.

"That's nutty," he said.

Suddenly she remembered why she was here! Just because she had nearly seen him totally naked was no reason to get off track. He was desperately alone in the world! She was here to save him from himself.

"So what if it's nutty?" she said, lifting her chin. "Does everything have to be sane? Does everything have to be on a schedule? Does everything have to be under your control?"

Coming from her, who had always been the perfect one, that was quite funny. But he didn't have to know it was out of character for her. Besides, what had all her efforts to be perfect ever gotten her?

She had spent so much time and effort and energy trying to be the perfect daughter. And then the perfect fiancée. What had it made her?

Perfectly forgettable. Perfectly disposable.

"You sound like my sister," he said, not happily.

"Can't you be spontaneous?"

He glared at her. "I can be as spontaneous as the next guy."

"So prove it. For the greater good," she reminded him.

"Please don't say it. Please."

"What?"

"Kettle Bend needs you."

"I won't say it. But come to the dog park. One hour. It's really part of your agreement to participate in the interview. I've even got it down from four interviews to one. I helped you out in your moment of need. With your nephews."

She had used every argument she had. He seemed unmoved by all of them.

"I think your being the cause of my public nakedness should clear all my debts."

"Nobody saw you," she said hastily. "And I didn't look!"

His lips twitched. Something shifted, ever so slightly. Whatever it was, it was far more dangerous than his remoteness.

"Were you tempted?" he asked softly.

She stared at him. His eyes were wicked. This was the problem with deciding to rescue a man like him.

It was akin to a naive virgin boarding a pirate vessel and demanding the captain lay down his sword for her because she thought she knew what was best for him.

It was a dangerous game she was playing, and the mocking look on his face made her very aware of it.

She took a step backward. "Sorry," she said. "Obviously this was a bad idea. One of my many. According to you." She bolted to the bottom of the steps, then stopped to unwrap the leash from around her ankles.

"Oh, wait a minute."

She turned back to him. He ran a hand through his hair, looked away from her and then looked back at her. "Okay. An hour. To bond with the dog."

Sullivan closed his bedroom door, leaned on it and drew in a deep breath. Sarah McDougall was in his living room. With a dog. Waiting for him to throw on a shirt so they could go bond.

Him and the dog, or him and her?

"You could have said no," he told himself.

But as she had pointed out, it would be unreasonable for him to say no when she had come so willingly to his rescue when Jet had been destroying his sister's house, and Ralf had put on his marathon crying jag.

Who cares if he appeared unreasonable?

She'd seen him naked. And not under the pleasant kind of circumstances that might have been normal for a gal to see a guy naked, either. That was a good enough reason to say no.

But her face when he'd asked her if she'd been

tempted to peek at him had been so funny. He *liked* teasing her.

Besides, after their interview in the coffee shop, where she had left in a fit of pique, it had taken a certain amount of bravery for her to show up here.

Also, he'd since given in to that desire to probe her secrets. Not surprisingly, she was every bit as wholesome as she appeared to be. She'd never even had a traffic ticket.

Sarah wasn't a member of any social networking website, which was both disappointing in terms of a fact-finding mission and revealing in terms of the type of person she was.

But there were plenty of other ways to find out things about a person. An internet search of her name had brought up the Summer Fest website. The four-day extravaganza of small-town activity—games, picnics, bandstand events—seemed like more, way more, than one person could take on.

But he wasn't interested in her recent activities.

So he'd followed the thread to articles she had written for *Today's Baby*.

He read three or four of her articles, amazed that, despite the content, they held his interest completely. As a writer, Sarah was funny, original and talented. Which meant he'd been entirely correct in assuming some personal catastrophe had made her leave her successful life in New York behind.

Knowing those little tidbits of information about her made it difficult to send her away now.

She'd had disappointments in her life. It was possible, given the unrealistic scope of Summer Fest, she was setting herself up for another one.

So, as much as Sullivan thought spending time with Sarah McDougall had all kinds of potential for catastrophe, he could not help but admire her bravery. No matter how much he wanted to keep his distance from her, he couldn't throw that bravery back in her face.

He had been aware he'd hurt her at the coffee shop, maybe said too much and too harshly.

And so when he'd come back to his door after pulling on his jeans, with every intention of repeating the first message he'd ever given her, *leave me alone*, he'd been stunned to find he couldn't do it.

Those eyes on his face, embarrassed, eager, hopeful, ultimately brave.

Trusting something in him. Something he had lost sight of in himself a long, long time ago.

"This is really dumb, Sullivan," he told himself after he'd put on a shirt and some socks and some shoes, and opened his bedroom door to rejoin her.

He came down the hallway and saw her perched on the edge of his couch. Today she was wearing some kind of stretch pants that molded her rather extraordinary legs and derriere. She had on a T-shirt—with a cause, of course, breast cancer research, because she was the kind of girl who was going to save the world. Her curly hair had been tamed again, today, pulled back into a ponytail. Once again she didn't have on any makeup.

He could see a faint scattering of freckles across her nose.

She looked about twelve years old.

It reminded him again, that there was something about her, despite her heartaches, that was fresh and innocent, eager about the world.

Which was part of what made saying *yes* to an outing with her so damned dumb, even if it was fun to tease her. Even if it was hard to say no to the brave part of her that trusted him.

He should have sucked it up and done what needed to be done.

But he hadn't.

So now he might as well just give himself over to the mistake and make sure it was a glorious one.

She turned to him with a faint smile. "What's your decor inspiration? Al Capone's prison cell?"

He realized she was bringing elements of the unexpected into his carefully controlled world and it was unexpectedly refreshing. Despite himself, he wanted to see what would happen next.

How much damage could she do to his world in an hour, after all?

And how much damage could *he* do to *her* in just an hour? He'd give himself that. Like a gift, an hour with her, just enjoying her, enjoying the spontaneity of it, since she had challenged him about his ability to be spontaneous.

Who knew? He might even enjoy the dog.

Then he'd give her the gift of never doing it again.

"Al Capone had naked girl pictures in his prison cell," he told her, straight-faced.

A faint blush moved up her cheeks. He liked that. Who blushed anymore?

"You can't know that," she said firmly.

"It's an educated guess."

"I think we've had quite enough naked stuff for one day." She had a prim look on her face, like a schoolteacher.

He was astonished when, this time, the blush was his. He turned quickly from her and opened the door.

"Walking or driving?" he asked.

"Walking. He's not car-trained." She did stop at her car, though, and retrieved a large handbag from it. Her car was somehow exactly what he had known it would be: a little red Bug. Evidence of the dog and the tissue box filled the backseat, though.

After watching her struggle down the sidewalk with the dog for a few minutes, Sullivan realized the dog wasn't trained in any way, shape or form. He took the leash from her.

"Let me do that."

He did not miss her smile of satisfaction. Bonding-101 taking place according to her schedule of sunshine and light.

The funny thing was, he did feel a little twinge of pure optimism. It was a beautiful day. He liked walking with her, their shoulders nearly touching, her ponytail swinging in the breeze, her scent as light and happy as the day.

"For practicality purposes, we should name the dog," she said. "Just for today."

Sullivan cast her a glance. Oh, she was trying to wiggle by his every defense. Naming the dog would be dangerously close to encouraging an attachment to it. He could see clearly, she was that kind of girl.

If you gave her an inch, she would want a mile!

"He doesn't need a name for an hour outing."

"Just something simple, like Pal or Buddy."

"No."

"It's practical. What are we going to say at the dog park after we throw him a stick? Fetch, black-dog-with-big-feet?"

"Okay," he conceded. "It."

"We're not calling him It."

We're.

"K-9, then."

"That's not very personal," she argued.

"It's more personal than It."

That earned him a little punch on his shoulder. The smallest of gestures, and yet strangely intimate, playful, an invitation to cross a bridge from acquaintances to something more.

Don't do it, he ordered himself, but he switched the dog leash to his other hand, and gave her shoulder a nudge with his own fist.

He was rewarded with a giggle as pure as a mountain brook tumbling over rocks.

There were no other dogs at the dog park, which he thought was probably a good thing given that K-9 was very badly behaved. She said she was disappointed that K-9 wasn't going to make any friends.

He wasn't at all sure dogs made friends. He could say something about her Disneyland town and her rose-colored vision of the world, remind her of his cynicism, remind her of how different they were.

But, surprised at himself, he chose not to.

One hour. He could be a nice guy for one hour.

Sarah was rummaging in the bag and came out with a bright pink Frisbee. He could object to the color, but why bother? It was only an hour.

He took the Frisbee from her when she offered it to him, waved it in front of K-9's nose and then tossed it. The dog looked after the Frisbee, then wandered off to pee on a shrub.

"No friends, and he doesn't know how to play," she said sadly.

For a moment, Sullivan was tempted to say on the scale of human tragedy, it hardly rated. It could be the story of his own life. But again, he refrained. Instead, he went after the Frisbee and tossed it back at her.

Sarah leapt in the air, clapped her hands at it, and missed catching it by a mile. But when she jumped up like that he caught a glimpse of the world's cutest belly button. He made her jump even higher for the Frisbee the next time!

She couldn't throw, and she couldn't catch, either.

But she was game. Running after the Frisbee, jumping, throwing herself on the ground after it, making wild throws back at him. Her enthusiasm for life could be contagious! And if it was only for an hour, why not?

"Has anybody ever told you, you have the athletic talent of a fence post?" he asked her solemnly.

"In different words, I'm afraid I've been told that many times." There was something about the way she said it, even though her tone was flippant, that made him think someone somewhere had either told her, or made her feel, she didn't measure up.

There was no reason for him to take that on, or to try and do something about it, except that he had promised himself that for an hour he could manage to be a good guy. And that might include teaching her to throw a Frisbee. The world changed in small ways, after all, as much as large ones.

Isn't that what his sister had tried to tell him about Summer Fest?

He brought the Frisbee over to her, and gave it to her. "No, don't throw it. Not yet."

He went and stood behind her, leaned into her, reached around her and tucked her close to him with one arm wrapped around the firmness of her tummy. Sullivan took her throwing arm with his own.

She had stiffened with surprise at his closeness, at his touch.

"Relax," he told her. She took a deep breath, tried, but it was as if her whole body was humming with tension. Awareness.

So was his. He was not sure what he had expected, but what he felt with her back pressed into his chest was a sense of her overwhelming sweetness, her enticing femininity. She seemed small and fragile, which made him feel big and strong.

Stop it, he warned himself. He was not going to give in to the pull of age-old instincts. He thought he should have evolved past, *Me, Tarzan, you, Jane*.

"Concentrate," he said, and she thought he meant her, but he didn't.

He guided her arm with his arm. "See?" he said softly, close to her ear, "It's a flick of the wrist.

Arm all the way in to your stomach, like this, then out. Release, right there."

She missed the *right there* part by a full second. He went and retrieved the Frisbee. He contemplated how he felt.

The physical contact with her made him aware of how alone he had become in the world. Aside from the occasional hug from his sister, and being climbed all over by his nephews, when was the last time he had touched someone?

There was an obvious reason why he hadn't. Once you let that particular barrier down, it would be extremely hard to get it back up. To ignore the part of him that ached for a little softness, a little closeness, a little company.

The smart thing to do would be to back off, to coach Sarah from a distance. But Sullivan reminded himself that if he was going to make a mistake he planned to make it glorious in its scope and utter wrongness.

So he went and conducted the whole exercise all over again.

He allowed himself the pure enjoyment of a man who was doing something once. He became aware of her different scents—one coming from her hair, another from her skin, both light and deliciously fragrant.

Sullivan allowed himself to savor their differences—the way she felt, like melting butter, within the circle of his arms. He could see little wisps of golden auburn hair escaping her ponytail and dancing along the nape of her slender neck. His arms around her felt so gloriously wrong, and as right as anything had ever felt in his life.

He liked *accidentally* rubbing his whiskers against the tender lobe of her ear, then watching her flub that throw hilariously.

He liked how the nervous thrumming of her body was giving way to something softer and more supple.

After a dozen or so attempts, Sarah finally managed a half-decent Frisbee toss. The pink disc sailed through the air in a perfect arc.

Neither of them noticed. She leaned back into

him and sighed, finally fully relaxed. He took her weight, easily, rested his chin on the top of her head, and breathed in the moment. He folded his arms over the tiny swell of her tummy, and they just stood like that for a moment, aware of each other, comfortable with each other at the same time.

The park suddenly looked different, as if each thing in it was lit from within. He could see individual leaves trembling on branches, the richness of the loam. The sky seemed so intensely blue it made his eyes ache.

As he watched the dog, cavorting, joyous, and felt Sarah sink deeper into him, he felt as if he had been asleep for a long time and was only now awakening.

The moment had a purity, and Sullivan felt contentment. He was aware of not having felt like this for a long, long time. Maybe not ever.

The dog suddenly seemed to catch on to the game. He retrieved the Frisbee and brought it back to them, wiggled in front of them, his tail fanning the air furiously.

"Look," Sarah said softly, "he knows he's our dog."

Sullivan could point out it was not *their* dog. But she had turned and looked over her shoulder at him, and there was something shining in her face that didn't give him the heart to do it, to steal the utter purity of this moment from her.

In fact, what he wanted to do was kiss her. To touch those lips with his own, to taste her while he was in this state of heightened awareness. He wanted to deepen the sense of connection they had.

But sanity prevailed. Wouldn't that make everything way too complicated? He wanted a glorious mistake, but he didn't want to hurt her. Not her heart. Her past heartbreak was already written all over her.

Instead, amazed by the discipline it took, Oliver gently released her and backed away from her.

Afraid he had become transparent, he turned quickly away.

It was time to go home.

But he had used every ounce of discipline he had to release her. There was none left to do what needed to be done. So, he went to get the Frisbee from the dog.

Sarah watched as Sullivan broke away from her, drank in the expression on his face as if she were dying of thirst and he was a long, cool drink of water.

She contemplated what had just happened between them. Her skin was still tingling where he had stood at her back, and she felt a chill where his warmth had just been.

He had nearly kissed her. She had seen the clearness of his eyes grow smoky with longing, she had felt some minute change ripple through the muscles in his arms and chest. She had leaned toward him, feeling her raw need for him in every fiber of her being.

Was it that need, telegraphed through her own eyes, her own body language, that had made him change his mind? Had she puckered her lips in anticipation of a kiss? Oh! She hoped she had not puckered!

"Hey, give that here!"

Sarah watched, and despite her disappointment at not being kissed, she could not help but smile.

The dog had apparently decided he liked playing Frisbee, after all. Only he invented his own version of the game, darting away whenever Sullivan got close to him.

That moment of exquisite physical tension and awareness was gone. But it seemed, suddenly and delightfully, like a new moment awaited. With a shout of exuberance, Sarah threw herself into that moment, and joined in the chase after the dog.

Sullivan was as natural an athlete as she was not. He was also in peak physical condition.

As if chasing the dog wasn't leaving her breathless enough, watching Sullivan unleash his power almost stopped her heart beating, too.

He was a beautifully made man, totally at ease with his body, totally confident in his abilities. It was hard not to be awed by this demonstration of pure strength and agility, Sullivan chasing after the dog, stopping on a hair, turning in midair, leaping and tackling. As he played, something came alive in his face that was at least as awe-inspiring as his show of physical prowess. Some finely held tension left him, and his face relaxed into lines of boyish delight.

What haunted him? What made this the first moment that she had seen the grimness that lingered in his eyes, that sternness around the line of his mouth, disappear completely?

"Sarah, I'm herding him toward you. Grab the Frisbee as he goes by!"

She let go of wondering what was in his past and gave herself to what he was in this moment. But of course the dog leapt easily out of her grasp, earning her a fake scowl from Sullivan.

"You have to cut him off, not jump out of his way. He's a puppy, not a herd of elephants."

"Yes, sir," she said, giving him a mock salute and jumping out of the puppy's too rambunctious path as he catapulted by her again.

"I fear you are hopeless," he growled, and then he threw back his head and laughed as she made a mistimed grab at the Frisbee when the dog came by again.

Sarah found herself laughing, too, as they both took up a frenzied pursuit of the delighted dog. She realized the moment of closeness they had experienced didn't seem to evaporate just because they had physically disengaged from it. Instead, as they chased the dog, their comfort with each other seemed to grow, as did the fun and camaraderie shimmering in the air, carrying on their shouts of laughter, the dog's happy barks.

Finally, the dog collapsed and surrendered the Frisbee. Sullivan snatched it from him, and then collapsed on the ground too, his head on the puppy's back. He patted the ground beside him in invitation, and of course she could not resist. She went and lay down, her head resting on the dog alongside his, her shoulder touching Sullivan's shoulder, her breath coming in huffs and puffs.

Clouds floated in a perfect sky.

"I see a pot of gold," she said, pointing at a cloud. "Do you?" Of course, seeing that was a reflection of the way she was feeling. Abundant. Full.

He squinted at it. "You would," he said, but tolerantly.

"What do you see?"

"You don't want to know."

"Yes, I do."

"A pile of poo."

She burst out laughing. "That's awful."

"That is just one example of how differently you and I see life."

He said it carelessly, and casually. But it reminded her that they seemed to be at cross-purposes. He wanted the barriers up. She wanted them down.

But she had a feeling she had won this round. She slapped him on the shoulder. "Don't be such a grump."

He looked astounded, glanced at his shoulder where she had smacked him, and then he actually smiled. "Oh, I see a force-feeding of a full serving of Crabbies in my future."

Future.

She was determined not to ruin this perfect moment by even thinking of that!

She was getting way too used to that smile, and how it made him look so boyish and handsome, as if he had never had a care in the world. It would be way too easy to start picturing her world with him in it.

What was happening to her? She had wanted to rescue Oliver Sullivan from himself, but she had not intended to put herself at risk! She had her new world, filled with jam and Summer Fest. Rescuing him had just been part of the new do-gooder philosophy that was supposed to fill up her life.

Only something was going wrong this morning. Because it just felt too right!

So she deliberately broke the connection between them. She retrieved her bag, pulled out water bottles. She sat back down beside him, deliberately not making contact with his shoulder again. She got her pant legs soaked trying to get the dog to drink out of one.

Then she glanced at Sullivan and was transfixed by the relaxed look on his face, taking simple pleasure of a simple moment, and she realized it wasn't as easy to break connections as she'd thought.

"I haven't felt this way since I was a kid," he said.

"I know what you mean," Sarah said, finally giving in to it, and savoring how this closed man was revealing something of himself. What would it hurt to encourage him by revealing something of herself?

"When I worked for the magazine, the girls and I would go on all these fantastic trips. We spent a weekend shopping in San Francisco. Once we went skiing in the Alps. I feel as if we were trying to manufacture the feeling that I'm feeling right now."

She stopped, embarrassed by her attempts to explain her surprise at the exhilaration that had come from something so simple as chasing a mis-behaved puppy around a park.

But was this glowing feeling inside of her from the activity? Or from being with him?

He reached over and gave her shoulder a squeeze that said, *I get it. I feel the same.*

She turned her head and gazed at his face. Really, it was mission accomplished. She had set out to rescue him from darkness and she had done it.

The echoes of his laughter were still on his face. They would probably be in her heart for-ever.

It would be greedy—and ultimately foolish—to want more.

But she did.

The hour he had promised her had been up half an hour ago. He'd bonded with the dog. He'd no doubt do great at that interview, the dog clearly worshipped him and it would show.

It had been more than she had hoped for.

For an hour or so, laughing and playing in the sunshine, with his arms around her, and chasing that fool dog, Sarah had seen Oliver Sullivan at his best, unguarded. He had been carefree. Happy.

"How come you haven't felt this way since you were a boy?" she asked, not wanting to know, *having* to know.

He hesitated, and then he said, "I entered law enforcement really young. I had the intensity of focus, the drive, the motivation, that made me a perfect fit for homicide. But dealing with violence on a daily basis is a really, really tough thing. Dealing with what people are capable of doing to each other is soul-shattering."

Sarah thought of the grimness in his eyes, the lines around his mouth, and was so glad she had been part of making that go away, even if it was just for a little while. Even if it cost her some peace of mind of her own.

He continued softly, "If people tell you they get used to it? They're either lying or terrible at their jobs. You never get used to it."

"Is that why you came here, to Kettle Bend, instead?"

He was silent for a very long time. He moved his hand off her shoulder. "I caught a really bad case. The worst of my career. When it was done, I just couldn't do it anymore."

"Do you need to talk about it?" she asked softly.

He snorted derisively, leapt to his feet. "No, I don't need to talk about it. And if I did, I wouldn't pick you."

For a moment, she felt wounded. But then she saw something else in his face, and his stance.

It wasn't that he was not trusting her. It was that he was protecting her from what he had seen and done.

"I took a year off," he said. "That's good enough."

She had a feeling it wasn't. That he carried some dark burden inside himself that it would do him nothing but good to unload. But his face was now as closed as it had been open a few minutes ago.

"So, what did you do for a year?" she asked him, pulling the dog's head into her lap, scratching his ears, not wanting those moments of closeness between them to disappear, hoping she could get him talking again. Even if somehow it was opening her up in ways that would cost her.

"I rented a cabin outside of Missoula, Montana, and went fishing."

"Did it help?"

"As an experiment, I would say it failed. Miserably."

"Why?" she asked.

"I'd say I had too much me time. Hour after hour, day after day, with only my own dreary company. It was time to get back to work. Della had moved here. She wanted me to come, too. I thought something different would be good."

"And has it been?"

"I miss the intensity of working as a detective in Detroit. I miss the anonymity. I miss using skills I spent a lot of years developing. On the other hand, I sleep at night. I get to watch my nephews grow up. And small towns have a certain hokey charm that I'm finding hard to resist."

But she had a feeling, from the way his eyes rested on her, he wasn't just talking about small towns having a certain charm that was hard to resist.

Though she hoped hers wasn't hokey!

Still, she could not help but feel thrilled. Sarah knew that today had been a part of that. Today, he had shared his life with someone outside of the small, safe circle of Della and her family. It had allowed him to get out of himself. To engage. To feel a reprieve from the yawning abyss of apartness that separated him from his fellow man. And she'd been part of that!

The problem with that? It was hard to let go of.

"I have to meet with the Summer Fest committees this afternoon," she said, not looking at him. She ordered herself to let go.

To say to herself, *Do-gooder, mission accomplished. Go back to your life.*

That was the problem with messing with this kind of power. Regaining control was not that simple.

Because she heard herself saying, her tone deliberately casual, "You know, in terms of the interview tomorrow, maybe you should come. It would give you a real feeling for the community spirit that is building. It might give you some ideas how to work Summer Fest into the discussion at the television station."

After his lecture to her about all the things Summer Fest was not going to do for her, she was nervous even bringing it up. She felt the potential for rejection, braced herself for it. Sullivan was probably way better at exercising control than she was.

He stared at her as if he couldn't believe she was going to try for another hour of his time.

She saw the battle on his face.

And then she saw him lose, just as she had done.

Because he ran a hand through the thick crispness of his hair and gave in, just a little.

"I have to admit I've been just a little curious about how you are going to pull off the whole Summer Fest thing. It seems like a rather large and ambitious undertaking for a woman who can't even throw a Frisbee."

She looked at him now, stunned. "You'll come?"

"Sure," he said with a shrug, as if it meant nothing at all, as if he had not just conceded a major battle to her. "I wouldn't mind seeing what you're up to, Sarah McDougall."

CHAPTER SIX

"I CAN'T believe you talked him into coming," Mabel Winston, chair of the Summer Fest Market Place committee, said.

Sarah let her eyes drift to where Sullivan was in deep discussion with Fred Henry, head of the Fourth of July fireworks team, and Barry Bushnell, head of organizing the opening day parade. She felt a little shiver of pure appreciation.

"He's even better in real life than he was on the video," Maryanne Swarinsky, who was in charge of the Fourth of July Picnic Committee, said in a hushed tone.

The whispered comment echoed Sarah's thoughts exactly. Oliver Sullivan was simply a man who had a commanding presence. It was more than his physical stature, and it was more than the fact he was a policeman.

He radiated a confidence in his ability to handle whatever life threw at him. He was *that* man, the one you wanted with you when the ship went down, or the building burst into flames. The one who would be coolly composed if bullets were flying in the air around him, if he had his back against the wall and the barbarians were rushing at him with their swords drawn.

But he had shared with her that he did not feel he had handled something life had thrown at him. Sarah shivered again, thinking how truly terrible it must be. *Wishing* she had been able to relieve him of some of that burden.

But she had noticed, as soon as he had entered the room, there had been a sudden stillness. Then all the men had gravitated to him and all the women had nearly swooned.

"Just look at the way that dog is glued to him," Candy McPherson, who was running the old-fashioned games day, said. "You know, maybe we should have a dog show. Just a few categories. Cutest dog. Cutest owner. That sort of thing."

There was no doubt, from her tone, that Candy had already picked the cutest owner.

"We already have six events planned over the four days," Sarah said. "That's more than enough. Maybe we'll look at some kind of dog event for next year."

Candy looked stubborn. "I could fit it into the games day, somehow."

"Is he going to take the dog?" Maryanne asked her.

Sarah glanced over at Sullivan again. The dog, worn out from his morning activities, or just plain worn out from adoring his hero, snoozed contentedly, his head on Sullivan's feet.

Sarah was amazed by what she was seeing in Sullivan. She wasn't sure what she had expected when he met the committee members. Cynicism, possibly. Remoteness, certainly.

But the playful morning with the dog seemed to have lightened him up. Sullivan looked relaxed and open.

Or maybe it was just hard to keep yourself at

a distance when you were surrounded by people like these: open, friendly, giving by nature.

Unaware how intently he was being watched, Sullivan reached down and gave the dog's belly a little tickle.

"In terms of the free publicity we're getting from him and the dog," Sarah said thoughtfully, "wouldn't that be a fantastic outcome? If he kept the dog? A feel-good story with a great ending like that would bring nothing but positive to Kettle Bend."

"Talk him into it," Candy said.

Sarah smiled a little wryly. "If ever there was a man you couldn't talk into anything, it's that one, right there."

"I don't know," Mabel said. "You talked him into coming here."

Suddenly, all the women were looking at her so intently, considering her influence over that powerful man. She could tell there was curiosity and conjecture about the nature of her relationship with the handsome policeman.

Feeling herself blushing, Sarah said, "Let's get back to business, shall we?"

An hour later, she was trying to pry Sullivan away from them.

Finally, they were back out on the street, the dog padding along beside them as if it was the most natural thing in the world for the three of them to be together as a unit.

"I have to admit, Sarah," Sullivan said, "I thought you were being way too ambitious with this whole Summer Fest thing. But those people in there are really committed to you. You've built a solid team. I think, maybe, you're going to pull this off."

"Maybe?" she chided him. She stopped, planted her hands on her hips, and glared at him. Of course, it was all a ruse to hide how much she enjoyed his praise.

"Don't hit my shoulder," he begged, covering it up in mock fear with his hand. "I'll already be sporting bruises from you."

"Take it back, then," she said. "Say, *Sarah*

McDougall's Summer Fest is going to be an un-mitigated success."

He laughed then. "Sarah McDougall, there is something infectious about your enthusiasm. You're even starting to get to me."

"Yippee!" she said.

His laughter deepened and made things so easy between them. She was astonished that this side of him, easygoing, relaxed, so easy to be around, was lasting. She loved how his laughter made her feel. Like the world was a good place, full to the brim with excitement and potential.

"I'm starving," he said.

She realized the hour she had promised him he would be away had now stretched late into the day. It was time to let him go.

"You want to go grab a bite to eat?"

Could it be possible he didn't want to let her go, either? Amazed at the joy in her heart, Sarah said, "I'd like that."

Like chasing the dog around the park, sitting at an outdoor table with him was really just the most ordinary of things. A guy and a gal and their dog enjoying a warm spring afternoon by having lunch on main street.

Except it wasn't *their* dog.

And they weren't really a guy and a gal in the way it probably looked like they were.

Although it felt like they were.

How could such an ordinary thing—sitting outside under an umbrella, eating French fries, feeding morsels of their hamburgers to the dog— make her feel so tingly? So wonderful and alive and happy?

Probably because the man sharing the table with her was about as far from ordinary as you could get.

They talked of small things. The ideas for Summer Fest, the weather, his brother-in-law Jonathon's recovery.

Then, out of the blue, he said, "Tell me about your job in New York."

"Oh," she said, uncomfortably, "that's in the past."

"That seems like a shame."

"What does that mean?"

"I went on the internet and read a couple of your stories for the magazine."

"You read stories by me?" she asked, astounded.

He shrugged. "Slow night for hockey."

"You read stories about babies?" she said skeptically, but something was hammering in her heart. She was flattered. Who had ever showed that much interest in anything she did?

"Don't read too much into it," he said. "Once a detective, always a snoop."

"Why would you go to the trouble?"

"Curiosity."

Oliver Sullivan was curious about her?

He took a sip of his coffee and looked at her intently. "You are really a very good writer."

"I was okay at it."

"No, actually, you were better than okay. Tell me why you decided to leave that world."

"I already did tell you that. My grandmother

left me a house and a business. It was time for a change."

"That's the part that interests me."

"It's not interesting," she said evasively. But now she could see the detective in him. He was trying to find out something, and she had a feeling he would not be content until he did.

He was trying to confirm the heartbreak part of the scenario he had guessed at, when he had made her so angry and she had stormed away from the café. Now, Sarah would just as soon end the day on the bright note that they had sustained so far.

"Let me be the judge of whether it's interesting or not," he said silkily. "Why did you leave the magazine and New York? Aside from the convenient fact you were left a house and a business. If you were perfectly happy, you could have just sold them both and stayed where you were."

Her flattery was quickly being replaced by a feeling of being trapped. "Were you good at interrogations?" she demanded.

"Excellent," he said, not with any kind of ego, simply stating a fact.

"Curiosity killed the cat," she told him snippily.

"I'll take my chances."

"Why do you care?" she asked, her voice a little shrill.

"It's a mystery. That's what I do. Solve mysteries. Indulge me. I'm compulsive."

"I don't see anything mysterious about it."

"Beautiful, extremely talented young woman leaves the excitement of a big city and a flourishing career. She leaves behind shopping trips in San Francisco, and skiing in Switzerland. And for what? To live the life of a nun in Kettle Bend, Wisconsin, devoting herself to unlikely causes, such as saving the town."

She could argue she had already told him she had more fun today than skiing in Switzerland. She could argue her cause was *not* unlikely.

Instead her mind focused, with outrage, on only one part of his statement.

"A nun?" she squeaked.

"A guess. I didn't mean a nun as in saying the rosary and walking the stations of the cross. I meant, like, er, celibate."

"Huh. That shows what you know. I happened to see a naked man just this morning."

He choked on his coffee. "Touché," he said, lifting the mug to her.

"I had no idea I was appearing pathetic."

"Anything but. Which is why I'm so curious. The boyfriends should be coming out of the woodwork."

"What makes you think they aren't?"

"You don't have the look of a woman who's been kissed. And often. And by someone who knows how." He smiled and sipped his coffee.

Sarah stared at him. "How can you argue with a man who can paraphrase Rhett Butler from *Gone with the Wind*?" she asked.

"Besides, you've already told me on more than one occasion. No dating. You're obviously aiming for cynicism in the love department."

She was simply unused to a man who paid such close attention to everything she said!

"Okay, here is the pathetic truth. I was engaged to be married. While I was picking venues, pricing flowers, shopping for wedding dresses, and daydreaming about babies in bassinettes, my fiancé was having a fling with a freelancer."

"The dog," he said quietly, and then to *their* dog, "Sorry, no offense."

Really, she had said quite enough. But something about the steadiness of his gaze encouraged her to go on, to spill it all.

"He was an editor at the magazine. I caught the occasional rumor about him and Trina."

"Which you chose to ignore," Sullivan guessed.

"It seemed like the noble thing to do! To ignore malicious office gossip. I actually put it down to jealousy, as if certain people could not stand my happiness."

He shook his head. "An optimist thinks that light at the end of the tunnel is the sun," he said. "A cynic knows it's a train."

"It was a train," she agreed sadly. "I saw them together having coffee. It could have been business. I wanted to believe it was business, but there was just something about it. They just seemed a little too cozy, leaning in toward each other, so intent they never even saw me walking by the window. So I confronted him. Right until the moment I saw his face, I held out hope there would be an explanation for it. It was really just too awkward after that. I couldn't stay on the magazine and see him every day."

He was quiet, watching her intently.

"There? You wanted to know about my tawdry past, and now you do. You were right. I moved here to lick my wounds. I moved here because I felt I couldn't hold my head up in the office anymore. Are you happy?"

"Actually, I'd be happy if I could meet him, just once."

"And do what?" she asked, wide-eyed.

He shrugged, but there was something so fierce

and so protective in his glance at her that a shiver went up and down her spine.

After a moment, Sullivan said, "You know what really bugs me? It's that you felt you couldn't hold your head up. As if *you'd* done something wrong."

"I was naive!"

"That's not a criminal offense."

"From the expert on criminal offenses," she said, trying to maintain some sense of humor, some sense of dignity now that she'd laid herself bare before him.

"You understand that it's entirely about him, right? It has nothing to do with you?"

"It has everything to do with me. My whole life went down the drain!"

"The career you chose to let go of, apparently, probably not your best decision ever. But him? You were lucky you saw them together. You were saved from making a horrible mistake."

That was true. If she had not found out, would he have carried on, married her anyway?

It occurred to her, if she had married Mike, she might not be sitting here.

Even leaving her career—which Sullivan said was not her best decision—if she had not done that, she would not be sitting here.

Across from him.

Falling in love with the way the sun looked on his hair, and the way his hands closed around a coffee cup, and the way his eyes were so intent on her.

"I'm going to guess you started telling yourself all kinds of lies after it happened," he said. "Like that you weren't pretty enough. Or interesting enough. Somehow, you made it your fault, didn't you?"

Falling in love with the way he had of saying things, of making things that had been foggy suddenly very, very clear.

"It's one hundred percent about him, Sarah. He's a snake. You didn't deserve that."

"Well, whether I deserved it or not, it made me

cynical. Confirmed my cynicism about love and happy ever after."

He laughed softly. "You may think you are cynical, and you may want to be cynical, but, Sarah, take it from one who has that particular flaw of human nature down to an art form, you aren't."

"Well, about matters of the heart I am cynical."

"You didn't come from one of those postcard families, did you?"

Falling in love with the way he *saw* her, and stripped her of the secrets that held her prisoner.

"What makes you say that?"

"Something you said when we were playing Frisbee. I got the impression you'd been told once too often you didn't measure up."

Sarah gulped. He really did see way, way too much. He read people and situations with an almost terrifying accuracy.

Yet there was something very freeing about being seen.

"If you'd had proper support through your

breakup, you'd probably still be in New York writing. You probably wouldn't have decided to love a town instead of a man quite so quickly."

She stared at him, but then sighed, resigned to the fact he could read her so clearly.

"I actually did think I had a perfect family," she confessed, and confession felt good, even though she had already said more than enough for one day! "Except for the fact my father seemed to want a boy, it was a fairly happy childhood."

"Personally, I think that's a pretty big fact," he said, "but go on."

"When I was eleven, my mother discovered my father was having an affair. They tried to patch it up, but the trust was gone. There were two bitter years of fighting and sniping and accusations."

"And you'd come spend summers at Grandma's house, and dream of the perfect family," he guessed softly.

"I'd plot how to fix the one I had," she admitted with a reluctant smile. "It didn't work. When my dad finally did leave, he never looked back.

He remarried and his new family—two little boys—was everything to him. You wouldn't have even known he had a daughter from a previous relationship. His idea of parenting was support cheques and a card on my birthday. Despite his neglect, according to my mother, I started looking to replace him the minute he left. Then I did find one just like him—and nearly married him, too. Amazing, huh?"

"Not so amazing," he said softly.

She was suddenly embarrassed that she had said so much, revealed so much about herself, even if it did feel good to be so transparent. "It's a good thing I never committed any crimes," she said. "You'd have a full signed confession in front of you!"

The talk turned to lighter things, and finally Sullivan called for the bill, giving her *a look* when she offered to pay half of it.

As they walked back to his house, he charmed her with a funny story about his nephew Jet.

As grateful as she was for the change of subject, Sarah was aware of feeling dissatisfied.

He had uncovered her deepest secrets with ease, made her feel backed into a corner until she had no choice but to spit it out. Well, maybe that wasn't so surprising. That's what detectives did, right?

But now, after hinting this morning at the dissatisfactions that had brought him to Kettle Bend, he was giving nothing in return. In a way, he was keeping his distance just as effectively with the small talk as he had been with his remoteness.

Sarah bet he'd used charm plenty of times to avoid any intimacy in his life!

So, now they stood on his front porch, and Sarah was stunned by what time it was. "Shoot. I missed the vet's office. They're closed in a few minutes. I won't be able to get the dog back there in time."

She hadn't done it on purpose, but maybe the dog could wheedle by the defenses that she could not.

"Could you take him?" she asked. "Just for to-night? You have to pick him up for the interview tomorrow, anyway."

He shrugged. "Sure. No big deal."

Somehow she could not bear to say goodbye. Not like this. Not with him knowing everything there was to know about her in all its humiliating detail, and her knowing close to nothing about him.

"Are you from one of those good families?" she asked. "Or were you, before your parents died?"

He stared off into the distance for a minute. "Yeah," he finally said, slowly, "I was. I mean, it wasn't the Cleavers. We were a working-class family in a tough Detroit neighborhood. There was never enough money. Sometimes we didn't even have enough food. But there was always enough love."

He suddenly looked so sad.

"How did your mom and dad die?"

She blurted it out. Maybe because a dog getting by his defenses was not really a rescue at all.

Sarah watched him. She could tell he was blind-sided by the question. It was taking a chance.

But it just felt as if she had to move deeper.

Now he looked as if he might not answer. As if giving himself over to the simple intimacies of sharing a sun-filled morning with her and the dog had been enough of a stress on his system for one day. As if his peek into her life by going to the meetings and probing into her history at the outdoor café had been more than enough for one day.

But how was it any kind of intimacy if it was not shared? If it was a one-way street?

She held her breath, pleading inwardly for this breakthrough. For his trust. To offer him the kind of freedom from his past that he had just offered her.

"They were murdered," he said, finally, reluctantly, quietly.

She felt the shock of it ripple along her spine, felt the dark violence of it overlay the beauty of the day.

Then she realized that this dark violence must overlay him every single day of his life.

All day she had been watching him change, sensing his barriers go down. She had watched as he became more engaged, more spontaneous, more open. She had seen him reach out, take her secrets from her, expose them to the light of day, their power evaporated as the sun hit them.

But her secrets suddenly seemed petty, so tiny and tawdry in comparison to his tragic revelation.

The look on his face now reminded Sarah that the bond between them was tenuous, that he might, in fact, still be looking for an excuse to break it.

So even though she wanted to say something, to ask questions, or to say she was sorry, some deep, deep instinct warned her not to.

Instead, she laid her hand across the strength of his wrist, lightly, tenderly, inviting him to trust.

After a long moment, he said, "It was a case of being in the wrong place at the wrong time.

Mistaken identity. A gang shooting gone terribly wrong."

Her hand remained on his wrist, unmoving. Her eyes on his face, drinking in his pain, feeling as if she could take it from him, as if she could share his burden.

Suddenly he yanked his wrist out from under her hand, muttering, "It happened a long time ago."

It might be a long time ago, but it was the answer to everything. Why he had chosen the profession he chose—and more. It was the key to why he chose to walk alone.

She knew he had just given her an incredible gift by trusting her with this part of himself.

"Thank you for telling me," she said quietly.

He looked annoyed. Not with her. But with himself. As if he had shown an unacceptable lack of judgment for sharing this. A weakness.

But she saw something else entirely. She saw a man who was incredibly courageous. Oliver Sullivan had tried to take on something—or maybe everything—that was terribly wrong in the world.

But he had sacrificed some part of himself in his relentless pursuit of right. He had immersed himself so totally in the darkness of the human heart that he really did believe every light at the end of a tunnel was a train.

She had been right to come after him.

But now she could see if she had thought finding out about him would create closeness, the exact opposite was true.

He fitted his key in his door, shoved the dog inside without looking back at her. "I have to go."

Retreating. Saying no to the day and to what her hand on his wrist had offered. Saying he could carry his burdens by himself.

Even if it killed him.

Just when she thought he was going to leave without even saying goodbye, he turned back to her suddenly, took a step toward her and then stood above her, looked down at her with dark eyes, smoky with longing. He took his finger and tilted her chin up. And dropped his head over hers and kissed her.

His lips touching her lips were incredible. He tasted of things that were real—rain and raging rivers—and things that were strong and unbreakable—mountain peaks and granite canyons.

He tasted not of heaven, as she had thought he would, but of something so much better. Earth: magnificent, abundant, mysterious, life-giving, *attainable to mere mortals.*

She could feel a fire stirring to life in her belly. She thought she had doused that particular flame, but now she could see that wasn't quite right.

No, that wasn't right at all.

It was as if every kiss and every passionate moment Sarah had experienced before this one had been the cheapest of imitations. Not real at all.

She told herself it was a hello kind of kiss, a door opening, something beginning between them. That's what she thought she tasted on his lips: realness, and strength and the utter spring freshness of new beginning.

But when his lips left hers, she opened her eyes, reluctantly. He took a step back from her and she read a different truth entirely in his eyes.

His eyes were suddenly both shadowed and shuttered.

It hadn't been hello at all. It had been goodbye.

Then he straightened and smiled slightly, that cynical my-heart-is-made-of-stone smile.

"Sarah," he said softly, "you've got your hands full trying to save this town. Don't you even try to save me."

Then he turned and walked through his open door. He was alone, even though the dog was with him. He was the gunfighter leaving town.

Not needing anyone or anything. Not a woman and not a dog.

She was humiliated that she had been so transparent.

But then she realized, buried in there somewhere, in those soft words, had been an admission.

He hadn't said he didn't need saving.

He had just warned her not to try.

It seemed to her, suddenly, that in her whole life she had never been spontaneous, she had never done what her heart wanted her to do.

She'd always backed down from the desires of her heart, so afraid of being let down, of being disappointed, that she had not even spoken them, let alone acted on them.

Sarah had always chosen the safe way, the conservative way, the don't-rock-the-boat way. She had never broken the rules. She had worked hard at being the proverbial good girl.

Where had that gotten her? Had it ever earned her the love and approval she had been so desperate for?

No.

Except this morning, for once in her life, Sarah had done what she wanted to do, not what she *should* do. Because she *should* have obeyed his boundaries. But instead, she had marched up the steps of Oliver Sullivan's house with that dog, an act of instinct, as brave as she had ever been.

And today she had *lived.*

Somehow, after that, after having *lived* so completely, having experienced exhilaration in such simplicity, life was never going to be the same.

Taking a deep breath, even though she was quivering inside, Sarah decided she wasn't backing down now. With every ounce of courage she possessed, she crossed the threshold into his house, where Sullivan stood by his open door, just getting ready to shut it.

Tentatively, she reached out, touched his face. She felt the roughness of a new growth of whiskers under the tenderness of her palm. She touched the stern line of his mouth with her fingertips.

Something shifted in his face. She could clearly see the struggle there.

When she saw that struggle, she sighed, and pulled herself in close to him. She wrapped her arms around the solidness of his neck and pressed herself against the length of him.

She could feel the absolute strength of him, the soft heat radiating off his body. She could hear the beat of his heart quickening beneath his shirt. She could smell the rich, seductive aroma of him.

She held on tight, waiting to see if he would recoil from her, reject her as she had been rejected by her father. As she had been rejected when a man she'd thought she had loved, whom she had planned her future with, had cavalierly given himself to another.

Would Oliver Sullivan reject her?

Or would he surrender?

She was terrified of finding out.

But she was even more terrified of walking away without having the courage to explore what might have been.

CHAPTER SEVEN

SULLIVAN felt the delicious curve of Sarah's body pressed against the length of him. If there was a word that was not in his vocabulary, it was this one.

Rest.

From the moment he had first met her, everything about her had told him she would offer him this.

A place in the world where he could rest.

Where he could lay down his shield, and share his burdens, and rest his weary, weary heart. Where he could find peace.

He had tried to send her away, he had tried to save her from himself. And instead of going, she had seen right through him, to what he needed most of all.

He was taken by her bravery all over again.

And by his own lack of it. Because he should have refused what she was offering him and he could not.

Instead, he kissed the top of her head and pulled her in close to him. She stirred against him and looked up at him, and there were tears shining in her eyes.

So, instead of doing what he needed to do— putting her away from him and shutting the door on her—he touched his fingers to her tears and then touched those fingers to his lips.

"Don't cry, sweet Sarah," he said softly. "Please don't cry."

He realized he wasn't nearly as hardened to tears as he had thought he was. Because he wanted never to be the reason for her tears.

"What do you want?" he asked, into her hair.

"I want this day to never end," she said.

He thought maybe he couldn't give her every-thing she wanted. In fact, he knew he could not give her the dreams that shone in her eyes: a perfect family, behind a white picket fence.

She was a nice girl who deserved a nice life. He did not perceive himself as any kind of nice person. Giving someone a nice life, given the darkness of his own soul, was probably out of the question.

But he could probably give her this one thing: a day that never ended. When he had first met her, he had thought he could spare ten minutes for her. Then this morning, he'd thought an hour with her would not pose any kind of threat to either of them.

Now, he considered. He could give her himself for the rest of the day.

He stood back from his door, inviting her in. "I hope you like hockey, then."

"Adore it," she said.

"Sure you do," he said skeptically. "Who's playing tonight?"

"The Canucks and the Red Wings, Game Two of the Stanley Cup Final."

He stared at her. Oh, boy. She was going to be a girl to contend with.

"Hey," she said, "you're looking at the girl who tried desperately to be the boy her father wanted."

"Do you know how to make popcorn, too?"

At her nod, he muttered, "I'm lost," and was rewarded with the lightness of her laughter filling up a house that had never been anything but empty.

And threatening to fill up a man who had never been anything but that, either.

The question *Where is this all going?* tried to claw by his lowered defenses. The question *How can this end well?* tried to force its way past the loveliness of her laughter.

He ignored them both. It was only the rest of the day, a few hours out of his life and hers.

What was so wrong with just living one moment at a time, anyway? Perhaps, one moment leading into another could get out of hand. Maybe it was a little out of hand already.

But it was nothing he could not bring back under his control the minute he chose to.

So they learned together that feeding popcorn

to a large dog in a small room was a bad idea. He learned she knew more about hockey than anyone else of his acquaintance. She insisted on staying until one minute past midnight, so she could say their day together had never ended. And he learned a woman falling asleep against your chest was one of the sweetest things that could happen to you.

Bringing things back under his control was obviously not as simple as choosing to do it. Because as he watched her putting on her shoes, giving the dog a last pet, he heard himself say, "Do you want to come to the TV station with me tomorrow?"

She beamed at him as if he'd offered her dinner for two at the fanciest restaurant in the area.

He watched her little red Bug drive away into the night and some form of sanity tried to return. One day was clearly becoming two.

After that he would extricate himself from this whole mess he'd gotten himself into.

The next day, the interview for television went

extremely well. The dog behaved, the questions were easy to answer and he managed to mention Kettle Bend and Summer Fest at nearly every turn.

Sarah was waiting in the wings, her face aglow with approval. It was a light that a man could warm himself in for a long, long time.

"I thought you said you weren't good at interviews," she teased.

"I guess it's different when you don't have a whole city howling for a crime to be solved, eager for someone to throw under the bus if an investigation isn't moving fast enough or moves in the wrong direction."

She wasn't just listening, she was drinking him in.

"Do you want to come to my place?" she asked. "We could order a pizza and watch Game Three together."

She wouldn't meet his eyes, so shy and fearful of asking him, that he did not have the heart to say no.

Besides, one day had already become two, so why not just give himself over to it?

The living room of her house was as he remembered it. A sweet, tart aroma permeated the whole place.

Sullivan remembered smelling it that first day.

And it reminded him of things gone from his life: cooking, warm kitchens, good smells. Home. *Rest.*

Thankfully, before he could get too caught up in that, the dog spotted her cat and went on a rampage, under the coffee table, over the couch and through the door to her kitchen.

He finally cornered the dog in the kitchen, where he was howling his dismay that the cat had disappeared out the cat door. Sullivan stopped and surveyed Sarah's kitchen, astounded. *Could anything be further from* rest *than this?*

He went back into the living room. Sarah was bent over, picking up flowers that had been knocked off the coffee table out of the puddles on the floor. Her delectable little derriere pointed in the air was somewhat of a distraction.

"Um, what's with the kitchen?"

She turned and looked at him, blushed red. Because she knew he'd been sneaking a peek at her backside or because Little Susie Homemaker did not like getting caught with a mess in her perfect life?

"It's my new decorating theme," she said, a touch defensively. "I call it Titanic, After the Sinking."

"It's more like Bomb Goes Off in the Rhubarb Patch." He turned back and looked at the kitchen. Every counter was covered in rhubarb, some of it wilted. There were pots stacked in the sink and overflowing it. In an apparent attempt to prolong its life, some of the rhubarb was stuck, stalks down, in buckets full of water.

"Just shut the door," she pleaded.

"Is that rhubarb on the *ceiling*?"

She came and stood beside him with her rescued flowers. "I had a little accident with the pressure cooker."

"People can be killed by those things!" he said, his tone a little more strident than he wanted.

"I just thought I could expedite the jam-making process. As you can see, I'm a little behind."

He turned and looked at her. He saw by the slump of her shoulders that she *hated* making jam. And he also saw that this was, at least in part, his fault. She'd been out with him when she clearly should have been making her jam.

So he closed the kitchen door, partly to protect the cat and partly to protect her from whatever it was she hated so much. They ordered a pizza and watched hockey—and learned you shouldn't feed all-dressed pizza to a large dog in a small room.

After the game, he really knew it was time for him to go.

But in a way, whether he wanted it or not, she had rescued him from his life. Only for a few days, it was going to be over soon, he told himself firmly, but he wanted to do something for her.

"Let's tackle that rhubarb together," he said.

Her mouth fell open. "Oliver, that's not necessary. I can manage."

Oliver. Why did she insist on calling him that? And why did it feel so right off her lips? Part of this sensation of homecoming.

Yes, he owed her something.

"Sure, you can manage," he said. "Just fit in a few thousand jars of rhubarb jam between saving the town, and—" And what? *Saving me.* "—and everything else," he finished lamely.

"I only have a couple of dozen orders left to fill," she said. "And then I hoped to have some ready for the Market Place at Summer Fest, but if that doesn't happen it's okay."

But it wasn't really okay.

She was putting her livelihood on hold for the town. And for him.

He could help her with this. Repay his depts. Then *adiós, amiga.* He would have given her—

and himself—two days, one hour and ten minutes.

"Show me to your recipe," he said.

"No, I—"

"Don't argue with me."

She looked at him stubbornly. It occurred to him he actually *liked* arguing with her.

She folded her arms over her chest. "I can argue with you if I want."

"Yes," he said, "you can. But I have to warn you, there will be repercussions."

"Such as?" she said, unintimidated.

"Such as my tea-towel snapping is world class."

"Your what?"

"Let me demonstrate." He took a tea towel from where it hung over her oven handle. He spun it, and then flicked it. The air cracked with the sound. He spun it again, moved toward her, then snapped it in the general direction of that delectable little backside.

"Hey!"

But she was running, and then they were darting around her kitchen island, and in and out of the buckets of rhubarb. They'd forgotten to shut the door, so the puppy joined in, not sure what he was chasing, but thrilled to be part of the game.

On her way by the stove, she grabbed her own tea towel, spinning while running. Then she turned and faced him, got off a pretty good crack at him. Laughing, he swiveled around, and they reversed their wild chase through her kitchen.

Finally, gasping for breath, choking on laughter, they stopped. She surrendered.

She showed him her grandmother's recipe.

"'Spring Fling,'" he read. Then he read the rest, and looked up at her with a wry smile. "You think this works?"

"Of course not!"

He looked back at the recipe. "No wonder you hate making jam," he said. "Sixty-two cups of rhubarb, finely chopped? You'd have to eat a couple of jars of the stuff first. You know, so you felt good and frisky."

"I don't hate making jam," she said stubbornly.

"And I used up all my frisky being chased around the kitchen."

"Yes, you *do* hate making jam." He was willing to bet he could coax the frisky part out of her, too.

But he wasn't going to. He was going to be a Boy Scout doing his good deed for the day.

Whether or not she hated making jam, another truth was soon apparent to him. He really did like the playful interactions with her. Friskiness aside, it was fun bantering. Bugging her. Chasing her around the kitchen until the dog was wild and she was helpless with laughter.

He really did like arguing with her about what was finely chopped and what was not. About training dogs. About whether or not to try the pressure cooker again.

It was two o'clock in the morning when he stood at her front door, putting on his coat and shoes. He doubted he would ever feel free of the smell of cooking rhubarb.

"Do you have to work tomorrow?" she asked, concerned.

"Yeah, I start really early. Five-thirty. It's okay. I'm used to rough hours."

"I can't believe it! All that jam, done. And the most fun I've ever had doing it, too."

Then she blushed.

And he realized he had never left a woman's house at two in the morning with *nothing* happening.

Except thirty-two pint jars of jam sitting neatly on a counter, glowing like jewels. Except chasing her around the kitchen, snapping a tea towel at her behind. Except standing shoulder to shoulder, washing and drying that mountain of pots.

Oh, something *was* happening, all right. It felt like he was being cured of the sourness of old heartaches. It felt as if he was feeling new hope.

Dangerous ways to feel.

He hadn't even eaten any of that blasted jam! Unless the taste test off the shared spoon counted. Unless licking that little splotch off the inside of her wrist counted. It was the best damned jam he'd ever tasted, but he was well aware that what he was feeling didn't have a thing to do with the jam.

It was the circumstances that had made it so sweet and so tart. If coming home had a taste, that would be it.

He straightened, looked at her, and just could not resist.

He beckoned her into the circle of his arms, tilted her chin up and touched his lips to hers. Then he deepened the kiss.

And found out he had been wrong about the taste of coming home.

It was not in her jam.

It was in her lips.

She took a step back from him. He could see the question in her eyes.

She bent and took the dog's ears in both her hands, and planted a kiss right on the tip of his black nose.

When she straightened, she looked Sullivan right in the eye.

"I think it's time to give the dog a real name," she said.

It jolted him. Because it wasn't really about giving the dog a name. It was about whether or not he could commit.

It was about his phobia to attachment.

It was about where this was all going.

He didn't answer her, and he could see the disappointment in her face.

He'd always known he was bound to disappoint her. The truth? Sarah McDougall didn't really know the first thing about him.

Now might be the time to tell her. He was damaged. He had failed at a relationship before. She'd made a poor choice in a man before, and he would be a worse choice.

But even telling her the details of his life and of his past implied this was all going somewhere, and he was determined that it wasn't.

So when Sarah said, "Do you want to meet after

work tomorrow? We can walk the dog-without-the-name."

He knew he had to say no. He *knew* it. But he didn't. The new hope that had sprung up in him, unbidden, wouldn't let him.

"Why don't you meet me at my place around four?" he said. "Don't come earlier. I don't want to get caught in the shower again." And he realized he liked to make her blush nearly as much as he liked to argue with her.

But she wasn't letting him have the upper hand completely. She smiled sweetly and said, "I'm going to make a list of names for the dog."

As he walked away from her, Sullivan realized two days were becoming three. His legendary discipline was failing him at every turn. No, not at every turn. Maybe it was to convince himself he was still in control that he decided right then and there that he was never going to name that dog.

"Trey, Timothy, Taurus, Towanda…"

"Towanda?"

"I just threw that in to see if you were paying attention. I'm already at T and I find it hard to believe you haven't liked one single name for the dog," she commented.

"Sarah, I'm not keeping him. It doesn't make sense to name him. That will be up to the people who get him."

He said he wasn't keeping the dog, but Sarah didn't believe him.

The three of them had spent lots of time together over the last week. That dog belonged with Oliver Sullivan and he knew it! He was just being stubborn.

And he was certainly that. Stubborn. Strong.

But what most people would not know was that he was also funny. Unexpectedly tender. Gentle. Intelligent. Playful.

Sarah slid a look at him. They were walking the dog by the river, Oliver's idea, to get the dog over his fear of water.

She watched him throw a stick into the water, and felt her heart soar at the look on his face when the dog refused to fetch. Determined. Curious. Open. Tender.

What was happening to her? And then, just like that, she knew.

She wasn't just in love with things about him: the way his hair fell over his eye, the way his smile could light up her whole world, the way he could make making a walk along the river or making jam an adventure in being alive.

She was falling in love with Oliver Sullivan.

She contemplated that thought and waited for a feeling of terror to overtake her. Instead a feeling of exuberance filled her.

Life had never been better. Ever since the interview that he had done, reservations for accommodations during Summer Fest were pouring into the town. The committees were going full steam ahead, and final details were in place for most of the activities and events.

Every booth was sold out for Market Place.

In the last week, Sarah had seen Oliver every day. They had walked the dog. One day they rented bikes and rode the entire river path, the dog bounding along beside them, a reflection of the joy in the air. The most ordinary of things—making popcorn and watching hockey—became infused with the most extraordinary light.

They had exchanged tentative kisses that were growing deeper and more passionate with each passing day.

They held hands openly.

When they watched TV he put his arm over her shoulder, pulled her in tight to him. Sometimes he would take her hand, kiss it, blow on where the kiss had been, and laugh when she tried to shake off the shivers that went up and down her spine.

But that had nothing on the quivers she felt every single time she saw him. Her first glimpse of him in a day always felt as if her heart had been closed, like a fist, and now it opened, waiting, expecting to be filled.

And he never disappointed.

As she watched, he threw a stick in the water

again for the dog. Spring runoff was finished. The river was shallow and mellow.

The dog whined, watched it plaintively, and then went and hid behind Oliver's leg, peeking out at the stick drifting lazily down the river. She watched the stick go, thinking about currents, how you could be caught in one before you knew it. You started out drifting lazily along, and then what?

He sighed, and scratched the dog's ears. "Aw, hells bells," he said. "Maybe I am keeping him." Then he turned and looked at her, gauging something.

"My sister invited us over for dinner tomorrow. Are you game?"

She stared at him. He might be keeping the dog. His sister had invited *them* for dinner. Everything was changing and deepening in the most exciting and terrifying of ways.

"Did you tell your sister about me?" she asked, something pounding in her chest. She knew from the way he looked when he talked about Della that his sister was the most important person in his world. What would it mean if he had talked to her about Sarah?

He looked sheepish. "Nah. She saw us riding bikes along the river path. She said she nearly drove into the river she was so shocked to see me on a bike. She thinks I don't know how to have fun. What do you think of that?"

"She doesn't know you at all."

He laughed. "She doesn't know what I've become in the last little while."

His eyes rested on hers with *that* look in them. The one that made her insides feel as if they were turning to goo, the one that made her heart feel as if it was expanding mightily, the one that stirred embers within her to flame.

"I'd love to go for dinner with you at your sister's house," she said.

He nodded, looked out at the river. "That's what I was afraid of."

She knew then that he felt it, too. They were

caught in something as powerful as the current of that river.

"Where do you think that stick will end up?" she asked him.

It was a dot now in the distance. She thought of it ending up in a green field a long way away, a child picking it up and throwing it again. Maybe it would make it to the ocean, drift out to sea, end up in a foreign land. The possibilities, for the stick and for her life, seemed infinite and exciting.

"Probably going to go over a waterfall," he said, "and be pulverized."

Sarah felt the smallest chill.

"I have to go," she said reluctantly. "Committee meetings. Are you coming?"

"No, I better go get ready for work."

Still, it amazed her how often he did come, it amazed her how quickly and effortlessly he won the respect of his neighbors, how he belonged.

She was aware that, more and more, they were

seen as a couple and couldn't suppress the thrill it gave her.

She walked into the meeting feeling as if she was still trembling from the lingering kiss he had planted on her all-too-willing lips down there by the river before they said goodbye.

"Oooh, look who's in love," Candy teased her.

Sarah had only just discovered it herself and felt embarrassed that she was telegraphing it to the whole town.

"I'm not in love," she protested, but weakly.

Candy just laughed. "Talk about a perfect ending to the story! Drowning dog brings beautiful couple together. And then they keep the dog!"

"Oh, stop, we're nowhere near a couple."

"Look, when you go to Hombre's on a Saturday night in Kettle Bend, and order one milkshake with two straws? That's official."

"You heard about that?" Sarah said.

"I even know what you were wearing."

"Stop it. You don't!"

"White safari-style shirt, black capris, and the whole outfit saved from being completely boring by candy-floss pink ballet-style shoes."

"Oh my God."

"That's small towns, Sarah. Everybody knows everything, usually before you know it yourself. So, you can tell me you're not in love all you want. The glow in your cheeks and the sparkle in your eyes are telling me something quite different. Have you named the dog yet?"

"No." But suddenly it felt so big, that she had to tell someone. She leaned toward Candy. "But I think he *is* going to keep him."

Candy laughed. "I never had a doubt! Like I said, the perfect happy ending."

The next night, Sarah met Della and Jonathon for the first time. Della had made spaghetti, and if Sarah was worried about awkward moments, she needn't have been.

Between Jet and Ralf chasing the dog through the house, and then making spaghetti the messiest meal ever, she was not sure she had ever laughed so hard.

Sarah was astounded by the level of comfort she felt in this house. Because Oliver had brought her, she was, no questions asked, part of an inner circle she had always longed to belong to.

Family.

Sarah marveled at the feeling of closeness. There was plenty of good-natured kidding around the table, but no put-downs. Oliver and Jonathon had an easy rapport, and he and Della obviously shared a remarkable bond.

Della asked her brother to put the kids to bed, while she and her husband did the dishes.

"You go with him, too, Sarah."

They went into the boys' bedroom together. There was a single bed on one side of the room and a crib on the other.

With the baby nuzzled against her chest, Jet propped up the pillows on his bed. Impossibly they all squeezed onto Jet's skinny little bed, she on one side of the little boy, and Oliver on the other. The dog tried to join them, and looked stubborn when Oliver told him no. Then he tried to crawl under the bed, and they all clung to the rocking surface until the dog figured out he wouldn't fit, and sulkily settled at the end of the bed instead.

Finally, everyone was settled and Jet carefully chose a book.

"This one," he said, and Oliver took the book from him.

Oliver was a great reader. With his nephew snuggled under his arm, they all listened raptly as the story unfolded. Within seconds the baby fell asleep, melting into the softness of her chest.

She stole a look at Oliver and felt a yearning so strong it was like getting caught in a current that you had no hope of fighting against.

If you had no hope of fighting against it, why not just relax and enjoy the ride?

She let his rich voice wash over her. She let the sensory experience flood into her: his dark head bent over his nephew's, his hand turning the pages.

After her relationship with Mike, she had tried to convince herself she could live without this.

Now she knew she could not. This was what she wanted.

No, it was more than that.

This was what she *needed*. This was the life she had to have for herself.

When the story was done, Oliver took the sleeping baby from her, settled him in his crib, Ralf's little rear pointed at the ceiling, his thumb in his mouth.

For a moment, they stood there, together, frozen in a moment of perfection.

Then they joined Della and Jonathon on the back deck sipping coffee and watching the stars come out.

"I never saw the stars in Detroit," Della said, and Sarah was aware of how the other woman's hand crept into her husband's.

Jonathon's leg was still in a cast, but if he had

any resentment toward Della for the fact he worked so far away, it certainly didn't show. He looked like a man overjoyed to give his wife the stars. Who would drive a hundred miles a day to do it for her.

The conversation was easy.

Sarah simply loved watching Oliver with his sister. Playful, teasing, protective. This was the real Oliver, with no guards up.

Later, she and Della sat at the table, the men had moved away to the back of the yard, the tips of cigars winking against the blackness of the night.

"How come you call your brother Sullivan?" Sarah asked.

"To tell you the truth, I'm amazed he lets you call him Oliver."

"Why?"

"He's never really been called Oliver. Even in school, he was always called Sullivan, or Sully."

"Even by you?"

"Threatened to cut my pigtails off while I slept if I ever told anyone his name was Oliver."

"Why?"

"Who knows? Somebody must have teased him. The school had produced *Oliver Twist* and he was probably tired of hearing *Consider yourself at home*."

For a moment, Sarah heard the jingle inside her head. *Consider yourself at home. Consider yourself one of the family...*

The feeling she had wanted her whole life. And had felt, for the first time, in the past few days.

"My dad always called him a nickname, Sun, *s-u-n*, not *s-o-n*. He said the day Oliver was born the sun came out in his life and never went back down. I was Rainbow, for the same reason."

Sarah felt the love of it, the closeness of this family, felt the full impact of the tragedy that had disrupted their lives.

"My mom called him Oliver," Della continued softly. "She was the only one who ever did. After she died, he seemed even more sensitive to people calling him that. I think it reminds him of all he lost that night. Which is why it surprises me that you call him that." Her voice trailed off, and she studied Sarah.

"Oh," Della said, and her eyes widened.

"Oh, what?"

"You're just good for him, that's all. I couldn't believe that was him, when I saw you guys riding your bikes by the river." Della looked out over the yard, a small, satisfied smile playing across her pretty face. Contented. "Denise wasn't good for him. Thank God they never had kids."

"Denise?" Sarah asked, startled.

Della looked surprised. "Oh! I would have thought he'd told you about his ex-wife. I'm sorry. I shouldn't have mentioned it.

Oliver had been married? And he had never told her? Sarah felt the shock of it. Oliver knew everything there was to know about her. Everything. He knew about her childhood and her father's philandering and her poor choice of a man to share her future and dreams with.

Over the past days she had told him about dead pets, disastrous dates, her senior prom and her favorite movie of all time.

How was it she felt so close to him, and yet, when she thought about it, he still had revealed relatively little about himself?

A wife in his past? Sarah felt stunned. When she had first seen him with his nephews, she had concluded he was a man who would be fiercely devoted when he decided to commit.

Getting to know him, she had concluded he would be a man who would take *forever* seriously, a man incapable of breaking a vow.

She felt the wrongness of her conclusions slide up and down her spine, reminding her she had been wrong once before.

She had been wrong about Mike, not listening to the subtle clues he had given of his growing dissatisfaction with their relationship.

Hadn't Oliver been giving her clues, too? Not naming the dog, for one. For another, he had told her point-blank he was attachmentphobic.

Why had she chosen to ignore all that?

Charmed, obviously, by *this*. By being invited to meet his family. By long walks with the dog. By making rhubarb jam together and watching hockey.

So charmed she had deliberately not seen the truth?

Suddenly, in the quiet of the night, they heard a cell phone ring.

"I hope he doesn't answer that," his sister said.

But they both heard Oliver say hello, and Della sighed. "I'll bet it has something to do with work. And I bet he'll go." She turned and looked hard at Sarah. "How will you feel about that? Because that's what finished Denise."

Denise again.

Sarah was suddenly uncertain that it even mattered how she felt about it! But she answered, anyway, a little stiffness in her voice, "I've figured out his work isn't what he does. It's who he is."

Della didn't seem to hear the stiffness. She gave

her a smile that until that moment had been reserved just for Oliver, and then she gave Sarah a quick, hard hug that renewed her longing to be part of a unit called family.

But had that very longing made her blind? Just as it had before?

CHAPTER EIGHT

SULLIVAN listened to the voice on the phone. "You heard *what*?"

From the porch, he could hear his sister and Sarah laughing, and turned his back away from the compelling sound of it.

Della adored Sarah. He could tell. Is that why he had brought her here? Obviously bringing a girl to his sister's was a big step.

Akin to posting banns at the church, now that he thought about it.

Why hadn't he thought about that before? It was unlike him not to think situations completely through. Why hadn't he thought that both his sister and Sarah were going to read things into his arrival here with her that he might not have intended?

In that moment when they had climbed into

that tiny bed, on either side of Jet, Sarah with the sleepy baby cuddled into her chest, he had seen that same look on her face that he recognized from the first time she had held Ralf.

Whether she knew it or not, this is what she wanted out of life.

But what had shocked him, what had come out of left field and whacked him up the side of his head was this thought: *it was what he wanted, too.*

Suddenly, he knew what terrible weakness had allowed him to not think things through, to bring her to his sister's.

He had fallen in love with Sarah McDougall.

It was just wrong. He had nothing to bring to a relationship. He had seen and experienced too much darkness. Not just seen it, sought it out. It had seeped into him, like drinking toxic waste. It had made him hard and cold and cynical, as ready to believe bad about his fellow man as Sarah was ready to see the good.

A girl like Sarah needed a guy like his brother-in-law, Jonathon. One of those uncomplicated, regular, reliable guys, with no dark past. Jonathon was a third-generation orthodontist. Jonathon had learned as soon as he started breathing what family was all about: safety, security, happiness, routines, traditions.

Sullivan and Della had learned those things, too. But the difference was they both knew how those things could be ripped from you.

Jonathon knew Della's history, but he didn't *feel* it.

Jonathon didn't really believe that your whole life could be shattered in the blink of an eye. He didn't carry the knowledge that a man could not really control his world. Sullivan carried that knowledge deep inside himself like a festering wound.

Jonathon naively believed that his strength and his character and his ability to provide were enough to protect his family.

And Della? His sister was courageous enough to have embraced love even knowing life made no promises, even knowing happily-ever-after was not always the outcome, not even if that's what you wanted the most.

Sullivan did not kid himself that he had anything approaching his sister's courage.

"Thanks for calling," Sullivan said, and clicked off the phone.

"Everything all right?" Jonathon asked.

"Not really," Sullivan said. He had known what had to be done before the phone call. He had known as soon as he had sat on that bed beside Sarah, reading stories to his nephews. He had known as soon as he acknowledged the truth.

He had to say goodbye to her.

The phone call had just given him a way to do it. Bradley Moore had found out Sullivan was keeping the dog.

Only one person in the world had known that. One.

His anger was real. But this was the part he couldn't let her see.

He wasn't really angry at her. No, Sullivan was

angry with himself. For letting this little slip of a woman slide by his defenses. For letting things develop between them when he had absolutely no right to do that, when he had nothing to bring to the table. He'd buried his parents and failed at one marriage already. In his final case as a homicide detective he had seen—and done—things that he could not forget.

This is what he brought to the table.

An inability to trust life.

Sarah sharing a deeply personal moment of his life with Bradley Moore, using it to her advantage, only confirmed what he already knew.

He couldn't really trust anyone.

Least of all himself.

Walking up from the back of the yard, toward the light, toward the warmth and laughter of the two women on the back deck, felt like the longest walk of his life.

Sarah turned and watched him coming across the yard, something troubled in her face as he came into the circle of the backyard light. As if she knew something was shifting in him, between them.

He had come to like how Sarah looked at him, lighting up as if the sun had come up in her world. The way she was looking at him now, tentatively, as if she was trying to decide something, made him aware he was already missing that other look, the one a man could find himself living for.

But a man had to deserve that. He would have to prove himself worthy of it every day.

A man would want to protect her from anything bad ever happening.

And because of what he had dealt with every single day of his working life, Sullivan knew that was an impossible task. He could not even protect her from himself, let alone forces out of his control.

Well, yes, he could protect her from himself. By doing what needed to be done. He took a deep breath and walked up the stairs.

"Sarah, we have to go." He heard the tightness in his own voice.

So did Della. So did Sarah. He saw it register, instantly, with both of them that something was wrong. He hardened himself to the concern on their faces.

"Sorry, Della. A nice night, thank you."

He whistled for the dog, who came groggily out of the boys' room. When it looked like Sarah intended to linger over goodbyes, he cut her short, took her by the elbow and hustled her out to the car.

It occurred to Sarah that the coldness wafting off Oliver like a fast-approaching Arctic front was being directed at her. She jerked her arm away from him. She wasn't exactly feeling warm and fuzzy toward him, either.

"What is wrong with you?" she demanded.

"Get in the car." He opened the back door and the dog slid in, looking as apprehensive as she felt.

He drove silently, his mouth set in a firm line.

She glanced at his face once, then looked out the window.

His expression reminded her of their first meeting. The barriers were up. *Do not cross.*

Sarah folded her arms over her chest and decided she did not have the least interest in mollifying him. Or prying the reason for his bad mood out of him! Let him stew!

Still, because his bad temper was crackling in the air around him despite his silence—or maybe because of it—her heart was racing. It felt as if the current she had been caught in was moving faster and not in a nice way. Swirling with dark secrets and things unsaid, moving them toward the rapids that could break everything apart.

Finally, he pulled up in front of her house.

His voice tight, he said, "That call I took at Della's was from Bradley Moore, the news anchor who did the follow-up story."

"I know who Bradley Moore is," she said.

"Of course you do," he said silkily.

"What does that mean?" she exclaimed.

"He said with Summer Fest just around the corner, how would I like to do one more interview?"

"That's good, isn't it?"

"No, it isn't. He wants to talk to me about my decision to adopt the dog. I've only told one person in the whole world I was thinking of taking that dog," he said quietly. "You couldn't wait to turn that to your advantage, could you? Your stupid festival meant more to you than protecting my privacy."

"How could you even say that?" Sarah asked, stunned. She hardly knew what to address first, she felt so bewildered by the change in him.

Her stupid festival?

"The facts speak for themselves. You were the only one who knew and now Bradley Moore knows."

It was his detective's voice, hard, cool, filled with deductive reasoning that she found hateful since it was finding *her* guilty without a trial.

Candy had told Bradley, Sarah thought, sickly.

But how dare this man think the worst of her? After all the times they had spent together, he had to know her better than that! He had to.

But obviously, he, who guarded his own secrets so carefully, didn't have a clue who she really was. Any more than she had a clue who *he* really was!

Bewilderment and shock were fueling her own sense of betrayal and anger.

"The facts do speak for themselves," she said, tightly. "And I've been mulling over a discovery of my own. Like the fact you have an ex-wife. When did you plan on telling me that?"

If she had expected shock in his features, she was disappointed. He looked cold and uncaring, his features closed to her.

"I didn't see any reason for you to know that," he shot back. "I don't really like wallowing in my failures."

"Is that how you saw the things I confided in you?" she asked, incensed. "Wallowing in my failures? I saw it as building trust. Apparently that was a one-way street!"

"Which was probably wise on my part, given where trusting you has gotten me! Imagine if I'd told you about my ex-wife, and the reason I left my job in Detroit. I'd probably be reading about my very worst moments in a sad story designed to bring more people to Summer Fest!" he accused.

"You are the most arrogant, pigheaded moron of a man I have ever met!"

"I already knew those things about myself. You're the only one who's surprised."

Sarah got out of the car regally. She was shaking she was so angry. She was aware they had squabbled in the past. Enjoyed lively arguments. This was different. This was their first real fight.

"Don't forget to take *your* dog with you," he said tightly.

"I can't have a dog," she said. "I have a cat."

"I'm sure they'll sort it out."

Should she read something into that? That

things could get sorted out? That if creatures as opposite as a cat and a dog could work it out, so could they?

Still too angry to even cry, Sarah opened the back door and called the dog out.

"Towanda, come here."

Inwardly she begged for him to comment that he didn't like the name. That he didn't approve.

But he just sat there like a stone.

She slammed his car door with a little more force than was necessary, and watched Oliver drive away.

Only when he was completely out of sight, did she finally burst into tears. The dog whined, and licked her hand, then got up and pulled hard on the leash, trying pathetically, heartbreakingly, to do exactly what she wanted to do.

To follow Oliver down whatever road he took her on.

"Have some pride, girl," she told herself fiercely.

He would figure it out. That it wasn't her who

had told Bradley. He would come around. He would tell her about his ex-wife, and why he had left his job in Detroit.

Sarah tried to convince herself it was an important part of their developing relationship to have a real disagreement, to see how they worked through things.

Soon she would know if they could pop out the other side of the rapids and float back onto a more peaceful stretch of water. He would apologize for jumping to conclusions about who had leaked his secret to Bradley. He would open up about his life before her, confide in her and tell her about his previous marriage, tell her about what had made him leave his job.

Failures, he had called them.

She hated the sympathy that tugged at her breast when she thought of him using those words.

He was a man who would not like to fail. At all. At anything.

She was sure he would feel better once he confided in her. She was also sure that something deep and real had happened between them and that he would not be able to resist coming to her.

But as days turned to a week, Sarah began to face the possibility that while she was waiting for them to come through the rapids, he was seeing them as already over the falls.

Pulverized.

There was plenty of proof in her house that things did not always work out. That opposites could not always find common ground. The dog and cat hated each other. If Sarah had contemplated that she might keep the puppy herself, a reminder of those sunshiny days of early summer with Oliver, a house full of destroyed furniture and broken glass from dog-chase-cat fracases was convincing her it was not a good idea.

Maybe remembering Oliver wasn't going to be such a good idea, either. There was no explaining the depth of her anguish when she would go to bed at night, contemplating that one more day had passed. He had not phoned. He was not going to phone.

Or bump into her by accident.

Or show up at her door with flowers and an apology.

It was over.

Sarah did the only thing she knew how to do to dull the sharp edges of the emptiness he had left in her life.

She buried herself in work, in relentless activity. She walked the dog six times a day, carefully avoiding places she and Oliver had taken him. If she hoped it would drain off the puppy's energy so he would give up on tormenting the cat, she was wrong.

She began to produce jam like a maniac, trying to ignore the fact that her kitchen had become a painful place, memories of them running around the island, snapping towels at each other crowded into every corner.

She attended every committee meeting, monitoring the progress of every function. She was helping build floats and stands for the market-place. She was putting up colorful banners on the parade route and picking up programs from the printer.

Despite the smile she pasted to her face, she felt sure everyone knew something was wrong, and everyone, thankfully, was too kind to say anything.

After spending the days trying to exhaust herself, every night with jars of freshly canned jam lining her cupboard, and the exhausted dog snoozing at her feet, Sarah sorted through the mountains of new requests delivered to her house from Kettle Bend City Hall.

It seemed all the world had watched the clip of Oliver rescuing that dog, and at least half the world his follow-up interview where he said the dog had not yet been claimed.

Now everybody wanted to adopt the dog. How was it that sorting through all these requests had fallen on *her*?

"Possession is nine tenths of the law," the city hall clerk had said, dropping off a sack of mail.

Some of it was addressed only to Kettle Bend,

Wisconsin. Feeling responsible for finding the perfect home for the dog, since she could not keep him, Sarah forced herself to read every single letter, even though it was ultimately as heartbreaking as the fact she had not heard from Oliver.

She, who was trying desperately to regain her cynicism about dreams coming true, seemed to be having the reality of her dream shoved in her face routinely. These perfect, loving families were everywhere.

They were in small towns and in big cities, on farms and on ranches and living beside lakes or in the mountains.

Photos fell out of some the letters. One sent a photo of the dog who had died and they missed so terribly. She read heart-wrenching letters from children saying how much they wanted that dog. She looked at crayon drawings of dogs. A dog bone fell out of one fat envelope.

She had to make a decision, for the dog's own good. He wasn't getting any younger. He was in his formative stage. He needed a good home. One without a cat!

But in her mind, though there were obviously many homes that fit her picture of perfection, in her heart he was Oliver's dog. She couldn't even stick with calling him Towanda, not just because it didn't really suit him, and not just because it would not be fair to name the dog in a burst of mean-spiritedness.

She could not name the dog, because in her heart it was Oliver's job to name him.

But she also knew she could not keep the dog from the family it deserved for much longer.

When Barry Bushnell called, frantic because the parade was days away and they still had not agreed on a grand marshal for the parade, Sarah gave up on her dream that Oliver would come around.

She had always, in the back of her mind, thought she could convince him to be the parade marshal.

She had always, in the back of her mind, felt she could convince him to love her.

What kind of love was that? Where you had to convince someone to love you?

To Barry, she said, "Let's make the dog the grand marshal of the parade. He's the one who got us all the publicity. Visitors would love to see him. And," she steeled herself, "on the final day of the festival, right after the fireworks, we'll announce what family the dog is going to."

"Brilliant," Barry breathed with satisfaction. "Absolutely brilliant."

But if it was so brilliant, Sarah wondered, why did she feel so bereft?

In fact, going into the final frenzy of activity before the parade, Sarah was aware that Summer Fest was going to succeed beyond her wildest dreams. Accommodations in the town were booked solid. The crowd was arriving along the parade route in record numbers.

With all this growing evidence of her success,

she was all too aware that she was plagued by a sense of emptiness.

On parade morning, the committee begged her to ride on the town float. But she didn't want to. Instead, she managed to lose herself in the crowd along the parade route and watched, emotionless, as the opening band came through, followed by a troop of clowns on motorcycles.

It was a perfect, cloudless day, not too hot yet. The streets had been cleaned to sparkling. Fresh flower baskets hung from light posts. Stores had decorated their windows.

Kettle Bend had never looked better.

She looked at the people crowding the parade route around her. It was just as she had planned it. Families together, children shrieking their delight at the antics of the clowns, grandmothers tapping their toes in time to the music of the passing bands. Candy apples and cotton candy—both Summer Fest fundraisers—were selling by the ton.

But as she looked at the Kettle Bend float,

Sarah was aware of fighting a desire to weep. All the people she had worked with to make this day a reality were on that float, smiling, waving. She had become so close to these people. How was it she felt so sad?

The truth hit her. You could not make a town your family.

She had learned that at Della's house. *That* was what a family felt like. There was simply no replacement for it. Love had perils. Love hurt.

And in the end, wasn't it worth it? Didn't it make you become everything you were ever meant to be?

Sarah felt the hair on the back of her neck rise, and she sought out the reason.

Standing behind her, and a little to the left, she saw Oliver. She was pretty sure he had not seen her.

Like her, he had chosen to blend into the crowd. He was not in uniform, he had a ball cap pulled low over his eyes, and sunglasses on.

He did not want to be recognized.

He did not want to play the role of hero.

He had never wanted to do that. She had thrust it upon him. She had thrust a whole life upon him that he had not wanted.

But maybe she had not completely thrust things on him. Why was he here today? Watching a parade did not seem an activity he would choose for himself.

Was it possible he missed the sense of belonging he'd felt when he'd joined her in the committee rooms? Was it possible he had read in the paper the dog would be the parade marshal? Was it possible he was reluctantly curious to see how it had all turned out?

Was it possible he wanted to see how it had turned out for her?

Of course, that would imply he cared, and the silence of her telephone implied something else.

Still, she could not tear her eyes away from him.

When a great shout of approval went up from the crowd around her, followed by thunderous applause, she glanced only briefly back at the parade route.

The dog was happily ensconced in the backseat of a white convertible, tongue lolling and tail flapping. The mayor was beside him, one arm around him, the other waving. The crowd went wild.

Then the dog spotted Oliver and jumped to his back legs, front paws over the side of the car, ready to leap. The mayor was caught by surprise, but managed to catch the dog's collar just in time. He pulled him back onto the seat beside him.

Sarah watched Oliver's face. She felt what was left of her heart break in two when she saw him watching the dog.

He took off his sunglasses and she could see the absolute truth in the darkness of his eyes. The memory of every single time they had ever spent together flashed across his face. She could see them throwing that pink Frisbee, feeding the dog popcorn that first night they had watched hockey together, and pizza the second.

In Oliver's eyes, she saw them chasing one another around the kitchen island, walking by the river, the dog cowering when he threw the stick into the water. In his eyes, she saw that last night they had spent together, saw them on the bed with his two nephews, the bed heaving up as the dog tried to get underneath it.

Oliver suddenly glanced over and saw her watching him. He held her gaze for a moment, defiant, daring her to *know* what she had seen. His expression became schooled, giving away nothing. And then he slipped the sunglasses back over his eyes, turned and disappeared into the crowd.

She stood there for a moment, frozen by what she had just seen.

The truth.

And she knew, as she had always known, that loving Oliver was going to require bravery from her. She could not hide from the potential of rejection, from the possibility of being hurt.

That day she had gone up the steps with the

dog, she had found the place inside her that was brave.

She knew it was there. She was going to have to try again. Laying everything she had on the line this time. She could not hold anything back. She could not protect herself from potential hurt, from the possibility of pain.

Real love had to go in there and get him.

But for now she had to let him go. The Market Place was opening right after the parade, and she had her booth to get ready.

Without staying to watch the rest of the parade, she, like Oliver slipped into the crowd.

The Market Place was both exhausting and re-warding. Throngs moved through it. Sarah had samples of jam for tasting on crackers, and be-tween keeping her sample tray filled and putting sold jars of jam in bags, she could barely keep up.

A man stood in front of her. Good-looking. Well-dressed. She offered him the sample plate, turned to help another customer.

When she turned back, he pressed a card into her hand. "Call me," he said, and smiled.

Once, she would have been intrigued by that kind of invitation. Now, she just gave him a tired smile and slipped the card into her pocket.

She actually was able to laugh at herself when she took the card out of her pocket later that night.

The name Gray Hedley rose off it, finely embossed. Underneath was the well-known logo for Smackers Jam.

Misreading men again, she chided herself. *Whatever he wanted, it probably was not a date.*

It seemed like a very long time ago, a lifetime ago, that she had mistaken another man's invitation for a date.

It was time.

It was time to find out if there was anything at all in her world left to hope for. When she had seen Oliver's face this morning at the parade, she had dared to think there was.

Now, dialing his number with trembling fingers, she was just not so sure.

She knew he had call display, and so she was both astonished and pleased when he answered.

He'd known it was her, and he had answered anyway.

"Hello, Oliver."

"Sarah."

Her whole being shivered from the way her name sounded on his lips. There was no anger there, not now. Something else. Something he was trying to hide.

"Congratulations on a successful first day of Summer Fest." His voice was impersonal. Polite. But guarded.

But she knew that the fact he'd even answered the phone when he had known it was her was some kind of victory.

She felt like she had so much to tell him. She felt the terrible loneliness of not having someone to share her triumphs and truths with.

"Oliver," she said quietly, firmly. "We need to talk."

Silence.

And then, "All right." Chilly. Giving away nothing.

Yet for him, just saying "all right" was a surrender. She hung up the phone and dared to feel a flicker of hope. That flicker felt like a light winking in the distance, guiding a traveler, weary and cold, toward home.

CHAPTER NINE

Sullivan watched as Sarah came up his front walk. She had brought the dog with her. He wished he had thought to tell her not to bring the dog.

On the other hand, she might read into it what he least wanted her to read. It was what he had known all along.

She might know then that he had become attached and she might guess the truth.

Attachments made a man weak. Love didn't make a man strong. It made him long for what he knew the world could not give, a way to hang on to those feelings forever. There was no forever.

Not for him. Over the course of his career he had seen it way too many times. Love lying shattered.

Maybe for her, if she found the right guy, like

his sister had found Jonathon, maybe there would be hope for Sarah. She could believe in love if she wanted. Yes, a nice orthodontist would be perfect for her. He should ask Jonathon to find her one.

Never mind that the thought of her with someone else made Sullivan feel sick to his stomach. That's what needed to be done.

He had always been that man. The one who did what needed to be done.

And he would do it again now.

He would send her away from him, back into the world where she belonged, where she could dream her secret dreams of wedding dresses and picket fences, babes against her breast.

The lie had not driven her away, the lie that he was angry with her about word getting out to Bradley Moore that he was going to keep the dog.

The lie had not done it. He'd thought it had. One day without her becoming another, the emptiness of his life made rawly apparent by her absence.

Then, always the brave one, she had phoned.

So he had no choice left. He had to count on the truth to do what the lie had not. He would show Sarah who he really was and it would scare her right back into her little jam-filled world.

He couldn't think, not right now, *but she doesn't like making jam*. He could not think one thing that would make him weak when he needed strength as he had never ever needed it before.

He opened the door before she knocked.

He hoped what he felt didn't show on his face. She couldn't know that he loved her little pink dress with the purple polka dots on it. She couldn't know that he wanted to smell her hair one last time. She couldn't know he had to hold back from scratching the dog behind its ears.

She could *never* know his heart welcomed her.

Sullivan took a step back from the truth that shone naked in her face. A truth more frightening to him than any truth about himself that he could tell her.

Just in case he'd got it wrong, just in case he had misread that look on her face, she said it.

She stepped toward him, looked into his face, and he hoped his expression was cold and unyielding. But if it was, it didn't faze her.

Sarah did what he'd come to expect her to do. She did the bravest thing of all. She made herself vulnerable to him.

"I've missed you so much," she said with quiet intensity.

I've missed you, too. It has felt like my heart was cut in two. But he said nothing, hoping it would stop her.

But she plunged on, searching his face desperately for a response. "Oliver, I love you."

I love you, too. So much I am not going to do what I want to do.

Because what he wanted was to lay his weapons at her feet. Surrender to it. He wanted to gather her in his arms and kiss every inch of her uplifted face.

But loving her, really loving her, meant he had

to let her go. He had to frighten her off once and for all. She deserved so much better than him.

"You'd better come in," he said and stepped back from the door, holding it open for her as she passed him. The dog was exuberant in his greeting, and that desire to lay it all down nearly collapsed him. Instead, he drew in a deep breath and followed her into the living room.

Seeing her there, on his couch, reminded him of the first time she had come in. The towel at his feet. Accusing him of taking his decorating lessons from Al Capone. Making her blush. The day that never ended.

He contemplated what to do next. Offer her a drink? No, that was part of the weakness, prolonging the moment of truth. This was not a social call. This was an ending, and the sooner he got it over with the better for both of them.

He sat across from her in his armchair. "I need to tell you some things."

She nodded, *eagerly*, that's how damn naive she was.

"I was married. In my early twenties. It lasted about as long as a Hollywood wedding with none of the glamour. I didn't tell you, because, frankly, I didn't see the point. I might share my history with someone I planned to have a future with. Otherwise, no."

He saw a tiny victory. She flinched. Some of the bravery leached from her face, replaced with uncertainty.

"You already told me your fiancé had a mistress. Well, I had one, too. That's what destroyed my marriage."

Her mouth dropped open with disbelief. Maybe he should just let her believe that, but then he remembered his truth would be enough to scare her off. He didn't need to make anything up or embellish anything.

"My mistress wasn't a woman," he said quietly. "It was my job. The work I did was not work to me. It was a calling that was worse than a mistress. It was demanding, it took everything I had to give it, and when I thought I had nothing left, it would ask for more. I was young, my wife was young. She had a right to expect she would come first, and she didn't. The work came first.

"This was the part she didn't get. For me, it was never just another violent ending. It was never just another body. It was never just another homicide. It was never just a job.

"It was dreams shattered. It was families changed forever. It was the mother who has been waiting all night for news of her son, and the young wife, pregnant with a child, who fell to the floor howling when she found out her husband was dead.

"To me finding who did it was my life. Nothing else. That's how I honored those who had gone. I found out who did it when I could. I lived with the agony of it when I couldn't."

He gathered himself, glanced at her, frowned at what he saw. She was leaning toward him, her eyes soft on his face, obviously not getting what he was trying to tell her at all.

"But don't you think," she asked him, "that

devotion to your calling was because of what happened to your parents? Wasn't every single case about finding who destroyed your family? Wasn't every single case trying to make something change that you never could?"

He stared at her. But if he looked at her too long, he would get lost in her eyes, he would forget what he wanted to do. He didn't want her insights. He didn't want her understanding. He wanted her to get that he lived in a different world than her. That she couldn't come over, and he couldn't go back.

"I've lived and breathed in a world so violent and so ugly it would steal the heart out of you."

Despite the fact she looked sympathetic, she did not look convinced that the world he had moved in could steal her heart. But that was because she was impossibly naive!

"I'm trying to tell you, each case is like a scar for me. Each one took a piece of me, and each one left something inside of me, too. Do you know how many cases I've been on?"

She shook her head, wide-eyed.

"Two hundred and twelve. That's a lot of scars, Sarah."

A mistake to say her name.

Because she took it as an invitation. She left the couch and came and sat on the arm of his chair, one hand resting on his shoulder, the other stroking his hair.

"Some people," she said slowly, "say a painting without shadows is incomplete. Maybe it's the same for a person without scars."

"I'm trying to tell you, you don't know me."

"All right," she said gently. "Tell me more, then."

Something was shifting. He wasn't scaring her off, and yet the words were fighting with each other to get out of him, like water bursting through a broken dam.

"On my last case in Detroit," he continued, re-lentlessly, needing to say all of it, "after thinking I knew the darkness of the human heart inside out and backward, I found out how dark my own heart was. In that last case, I came face-to-face with my own darkness."

He paused, glanced at her. All that softness. *Don't tell her*, he said to himself. *Spare her the supreme ugliness.* Just kick her out and tell her not to come back.

But he'd already tried that. From the very beginning he had tried to discourage her interest. The only weapon he had left was the truth, and he had to use it. He could not stop now. He was nearly there.

"It started like so many of them. Neighbors heard shots. Cops arrived, knew right away to call us as soon as they stepped in the door.

"You know what they found?"

She shook her head.

"A whole family, dead. The Algards wiped from the face of the earth. Mommy. Daddy. Five-year-old, three-year-old, two-year-old."

"Oh, Oliver," she said, and pressed her fist into her mouth. If he hoped she was finally starting to get it, the look in her eyes told him he was mistaken. She didn't get it! She still thought she could take some part of it, absolve him.

Why did it feel as if she was? Ah, well, she had not heard the whole sordid tale yet.

"We got it all wrong," he said softly. "We thought it was a gang war. We thought who else could do something like this? We thought they were sending a message to the whole community. Don't cross us, we run the show. Then a high-ranking gang member came to me, ridiculously young, given his status. But when I looked at that boy, I was so aware if Della hadn't saved me from that lifestyle, he would have been me.

"That kid was smart and savvy and a little cocky. Luke. Unapologetic about his affiliations. Said he'd been looking for a family all his life, a place where he could belong, and his gang was it. I can remember his exact words. *We're all just soldiers, man. Lots of kids gettin' sent over to the land of sand, killing people for less than what I kill people for.*

"And then Luke told me his gang didn't kill the

Algards. He was disgusted that we would think his gang killed babies, and I had offended his sense of honor. He told me I was looking in the wrong place, and he was going to find out who did it. And you know what? He did. He had contacts and inside channels and the power to intimidate in that community that I could never have. It was humbling how fast he found the truth.

"According to Luke's information, it wasn't a gang thing at all. The perp was my adult male victim's brother. It was a family squabble gone stupidly, insanely, irrevocably wrong.

"Luke said, *I can look after it.* And that's when I found out what a thin, almost invisible line can divide good and bad. That's when I found out the darkness was in me, too. Because I wanted vengeance for that family. For those babies gunned down before they ever knew one thing good. No first day of school. No visit from the tooth fairy. No first kiss, or prom, or graduation, or wedding. I didn't want to trust the outcome to the system. Two hundred and eleven previous cases. I knew, firsthand, things did not always go the way I wanted them to.

"*Twenty-four hours*, he told me. He told me if I hadn't looked after it in twenty-four hours, he would."

"You let him," she whispered, horrified.

Oliver laughed, and it sounded ragged in his own ears. "No, I didn't. I did the right thing. I brought in the brother. Complete confession. He killed his brother in a fit of rage over an argument. And do you know why he killed the rest of them, why he shot those little babies? Because they saw him do it. That's all. Because even that two-year-old baby knew her uncle had killed her daddy."

"So, you did the right thing," she prodded him.

"I guess that depends on how you look at it. Things did not go the way I wanted them to. He walked free and I could not stop thinking of those tiny, defenseless bodies. And thinking about him out on the streets. I could not stop thinking about the opportunity I'd passed on to have things looked after. Up until that point, I'd always felt like the cowboy, always felt like I was on the side of the righteous. But suddenly everything seemed muddy. Then it got worse.

"Within hours of beating the system, the brother faced street justice and it was swift and violent. I knew exactly who killed him. So I did my job. I brought in Luke. And it twisted my world up even further when he did not walk free. He was twenty-three years old and he got life in prison.

"You know what he said to me? *Worth it. We're all just soldiers.* Well, that was the end of me. I felt turned inside out. Who was the good guy? Who was the bad guy? I felt as if I had failed at everything I ever put my hand to. I failed as a cop, I failed as a husband, I failed as a son."

"Failed? You?" She sounded incredulous, still wanting to believe the best of him even though she had now heard the worst. She was still sitting way too close to him. Why hadn't she moved? Couldn't she see he was a man who had lost his moral compass? Who had lost his faith that good could triumph over evil?

"This is what people who have never been exposed to violence don't know. You think about it all the time. You think, *What could I have done to make it different*?"

"You can't possibly believe you could have protected the whole world!"

"No," he said sadly. "You are exactly right. That is the conclusion I have come to. This is what you need to know about me, Sarah McDougall. Other people have a simple faith. They believe if you are good only good things happen to you. They find comfort in believing something bigger runs the show. But I know it's all random, and that a man has no hope against that randomness.

"And that's why I can't be with you, Sarah, why I can't accept the gift of love you have offered me, or ever love you back. Because, despite having taken a few hard knocks yourself, you're still so damned determined to find good. You're a nice girl and I've walked too long with darkness to have anything nice left in me. In time, my darkness will snuff out your light, Sarah. In time, it will."

There, he had said it all. He waited for her to move, to get up off the chair, go to the door, walk out it and not look back.

Inwardly he pleaded that she would take the dog with her.

And then he felt her hand, cool and comforting on the back of his neck. He made himself look at her. But he did not see goodbye in her face. He was nearly blinded by what he saw there.

He had tried so hard to let her go. But she wasn't going. In her face, in the softness of her expression, in the endless compassion of her eyes, he saw what he had been looking for for such a very long time.

Rest.

Sarah stared at the ravaged face of the man she loved. Suddenly she understood the universal appeal of that video she had seen of him jumping in the river to save the dog. She understood exactly why that clip had gone viral, why so many people had watched it.

This man, the one who claimed not to believe in goodness, was the rarest of men. Here was a man willing to live his truth, a man prepared to give his life to protect someone—or something—weaker, vulnerable, in mortal danger.

She saw so clearly that ever since the death of his parents, Oliver had pitted himself against everything wrong in the world. He had given his whole life trying to protect everyone and everything.

No wonder he felt like a failure.

Could he not see that was just too big a job for one man?

With tears in her eyes, she saw another truth. Shining around him. He was willing to give up his life—any chance he had of happiness or love—to protect her from what he thought he was.

And the fact he would do that? It meant he was not what he thought he was. He was not even close.

"I have to tell you something, Oliver Sullivan," she said, and she could hear the strength and certainty in her own voice.

"What's that?"

He had folded his arms over the mightiness of his chest. He had furrowed his brows at her and frowned.

He looked like the warrior that he was.

But it was time for that warrior to come home.

"You are wrong," she said softly. "You are so damned wrong."

"About?"

"The darkness putting out the light. It's the other way around. It has always been the other way around. The light chases away the darkness. Love wins. In the end, love always wins."

"You're hopelessly naive," he snarled.

But she wasn't afraid. She was standing in the light right now. It was pouring out of her.

More importantly, it was pouring out of this good, good man who had given his whole life to trying to protect others and who had not taken one thing for himself.

Well, if it was the last thing she did, she intended to be Oliver Sullivan's one thing.

"I've lived it," he said, his voice tortured. "Sarah, I've lived it. It's not true. Love does not always win."

"Really?" she said softly. "What is this, if it's not love winning?"

She touched his neck, looked into his raised face, and then dropped off the arm of the chair right onto his lap.

"I love you," she said fiercely. "I love every thing about you and I am never, ever going to stop. I've come to get you, Oliver Sullivan. And that *is* love winning."

"You're being foolish," he said gruffly. He did not hold her, but he did not push her away, either.

"You think I would care about you less because of what you just told me?" she laughed. "You're the fool! Oliver, I care about you *more*."

She felt his eyes on her face, searching, and she

knew the instant he found truth there. His body suddenly relaxed, and he pulled her deep against him, burying his face in the curve of her neck.

She ran her fingers, tenderly, thought the thickness of his hair, touched her lips to his beautiful forehead, to each of his closed eyes.

"Let me carry it with you," she whispered. "Let me."

After the longest time, she felt him shudder against her, heard him whisper, "Okay."

And she finally let her tears of joy chase down her cheeks and mingle with his.

"Jelly," Oliver called, "Jam. Best you've ever eaten. Cures heartaches!"

"You can't say that!" Sarah chided him, but she was laughing.

He was helping her with her booth at the Market Place. It was the last day of Summer Fest. He had spent every minute since he had told her his truth with Sarah, something in him opening, like a flower after the rain.

They could not bear to say goodbye to one another.

They could not get enough of each other.

Last night, they had even fallen asleep together on her couch, words growing huskier and huskier as they had gotten more tired, finally sleeping with unspoken words on their lips. When he had woken this morning, with her head on his shoulder, her sleepy eyes on his, her hair in a wild tangle of curls, it had felt as if he was in heaven.

So Oliver Sullivan was selling jam—he'd donned an apron to get a rise out of Sarah—and he was having the time of his life. He didn't just sell jam. What was the fun of that? No, he hawked it like an old-time peddler with a magic elixir.

He moved amongst the crowd. He stood on the table. He kissed babies and old ladies.

He was alive.

How could it be that selling jam at a humble little booth set up in what was usually a school yard field could feel as if he was standing on top of a mountain? As if all the world was spread out before him, in all its magnificence, put there just for his enjoyment?

It could feel like that because she was beside him.

Sarah.

Who had listened quietly to his every secret and not been warned off. Who had set him free.

That's what he felt right now. Free.

As if aloneness had been his prison and she had broken him out. As if carrying all those burdens had been like carrying a five-hundred-pound stone around with him, and she, little Sarah, who probably weighed a hundred pounds or so, had been the one strong enough to lift it off of him.

"Excuse me, ma'am? If you'll buy a single jar of the jelly, I will show you how I can walk on my hands."

"Oliver!"

But the lady bought jam, and he walked on his hands, and Sarah laughed and applauded with everyone else. Plus, it attracted quite a crowd, and then they were sold out of jam.

"Come on, sweetheart," he said, putting the Closed sign up on her little booth. "We probably have time to win the three-legged race."

Later, lying in a heap with her underneath him, their legs bound together, nearly choking he was laughing so hard, he wondered if this is what it felt to be a teenager, because he never really had been.

The death of his parents had cast a shadow over the part of his life when he should have been laughing with girls, and stealing kisses, and feeling his heart pound hopefully at the way a certain girl's hand felt in his.

To Oliver Sullivan, it was an unbelievable blessing that he was actually getting to experience a part of life that had been lost to him.

The falling-in-love part.

Because that's what had been happening from the minute he met Sarah. He had been falling for her.

And fighting it.

Now, to just experience it, to not fight it, made him feel on fire with life.

Somehow he and Sarah managed to find their feet, and lurched across the finish line dead last. But the crowd applauded as if they had come first when he kissed her and they did not come up for air for a long, long time!

"I think we could probably win the egg and spoon race," he decided.

"I doubt it," she said.

"Let's try anyway. I like the ending part when we lose."

"Me, too."

Laughing like young children, hands intertwined they ran to the starting line.

For supper, they bought hamburgers with heaps of fried onions and then had cotton candy for dessert. They rode the Ferris wheel, and he kissed her silly when it got stuck at the top.

Then, as the sun set, they went back to his

house, briefly, and changed into warmer clothes and grabbed their blankets.

And their dog.

They joined the town on the banks of the Kettle River. People had blankets and lawn chairs set up everywhere. There were families there with little babies and young children. There were young lovers. There were giggling gaggles of girls. Young boys sipped beer from bottles, until they saw him, and then they put it away.

He and Sarah and their dog lay back on their blanket, and as the night cooled they pulled another tight around themselves.

The fireworks started.

It was exactly how he felt inside: exploding with beauty and excitement.

The dog was terrified, and had to get in the blankets with them, his warm body all quivery and slithery.

Sarah, one arm around the dog, leaning into Oliver, looked skyward, her expression one of complete enchantment. When he looked at her face, he saw her truth. He saw in her face she would always believe good things could happen if you wanted it badly enough.

And who was he to say she was wrong? She'd made this happen, hadn't she? The whole town and an unimaginable number of visitors were all sitting here on this warm night enjoying the breathtaking magic of the fireworks because of her. Because she had believed in a vision, trusted in a dream.

She had rescued him, too. Because she had believed in something it would have been so much wiser for her to let go of.

His way had not brought him one iota of happiness. Not one. Being guarded and cynical, expecting the worst? What had that brought him?

He was going to try it her way.

In fact, he knew he was going to try it her way for a very, very long time.

A firework exploded into a million fragments of light above them, and those fragments of light were doubled when they reflected on the quiet black surface of the river.

"I'm going to name the dog," he decided in a quiet place between the boom of the fireworks being set off.

She turned and looked at him, a smile tickling across those gorgeous, kissable lips.

"Moses," he decided.

"I love that. But why Moses?"

"Because I found him floating in the river. Because he led me out of the wilderness, to the promised land."

"What promised land?"

"You."

Right on cue, fireworks exploded in the sky above them, a waterfall of bright sparks of green and blue and red cascading through the sky.

She stared at him, and then she bit her lip, and her eyes sparkled with tears. She reached up and touched his face with such tenderness, such love, and he was humbled.

He knew he would not go back from this place

to the place he had been before. He might be strong, but he wasn't strong enough to survive a life that did not include Sarah in it.

"Marry me," he murmured, as the sparks of the firework faded and drifted back toward earth.

Her face was lit by those dying lights.

"Yes," she whispered.

As their lips joined, the sky exploded, once again, into light and sound above them. It was the finale: shooting higher, the sky filling with a frenzy of light and sound and smoke. And as the sound died, the fireworks disintegrated into pinwheels of fiery gold that drifted down through the black sky toward the black water.

Silence followed, and then thunderous applause and cheering.

To Oliver it felt as if the whole earth celebrating this moment. This miracle.

Of the right man and the right woman coming together and having the courage to say yes to what was being offered them.

Maybe all of creation did celebrate the moment

when that magnificent force that survived all else, that triumphed over all else, that force that was at the heart of everything, showed itself in the way one man and one woman looked at each other. Maybe it did.

EPILOGUE

SARAH came into the house, and smiled when she heard the sound. Banging. Cursing. More banging.

She followed the sound up the stairs to the room at the end of the hallway.

She gasped at what she saw. Where there had been worn carpet this morning, now there was hardwood.

Curtains with purple giraffes and green lions cavorting across them were hung on a only slightly bent rod.

Oliver sat on the floor, instructions spread out in front of him, tongue caught between his teeth, crib in a million pieces on the ground. Moses watched from one corner where Sushi had him trapped. She lifted her paw delicately to let the dog know who was boss, and his expression was one of long suffering as he flopped his tail at Sarah in greeting.

Oliver looked up at her. He had sawdust in his hair, and a smudge on his face. His smile did what it had been doing since the moment she said *I do*.

It turned her insides to goo.

"You know," he said, looking back at his instructions, trying to fit a round peg into a square hole, "I remember once I thought home was about rest. I was sadly mistaken. I haven't had a moment's rest since we bought this old junk heap." But he said it with such affection. And it was true. Everywhere in the house they had purchased together was his mark.

He had torn down every wall downstairs to give them a bright, open modern space that was the envy of the entire neighborhood, and especially his sister Della, who lived two doors down.

Oliver was not a natural carpenter or handyman. Sometimes he had to do things two or three times to get them right, sometimes even more. His work around the house involved much effort, cursing, pondering, trying, ripping down, rethinking and then trying again.

The fact that he loved it so, when he was quite terrible at it, made Sarah's heart feel so tender it almost hurt. This man, who had hated failure so much, had become so confident in himself—and in her unconditional love for him—that he failed regularly and shrugged it off with good humor.

That's what love had done for him. Made him so much better, so accepting of his own humanity.

She cherished that about him.

"You didn't have to start on the nursery just yet," Sarah said, and came in and ruffled his hair, flicked some of the sawdust from it. She had never tired of the way that thick hair felt under her fingertips. "We only found out we were pregnant two days ago."

"Ah, well, you know the saying. Don't put off until tomorrow what you can do today. I've been asked to consult on that case in Green Bay. You know me. Once I get going on that." He shook his head with good-humored acceptance of his tendency toward obsession.

She knew him and loved this part of him, still trying to make all that was wrong in the world right. But there was a difference now. Now, he came back into the light after he had spent time dealing with darkness. And let her love heal him.

"What if things don't go right?" she asked, tentatively. "It's a first baby. That's why I thought maybe you should hold off—" she gestured uncertainly around the room "—on all this."

He turned and grinned at her, that smile sweeping away her fears. "Everything is going to be fine," he told her, and his voice was so steady and so confident that she believed him.

Sarah marveled at the fact that Oliver, who had once had so many problems believing life could bring good, was already committed to a good outcome. He already saw a baby in this room and he already loved it with his whole heart and soul.

"I love the curtains. Where did you find that

fabric?" She went and touched it, felt teary that he could pick such a thing, that he could know it was just right. Then again, teary was the order of the day!

"Is the rod a little crooked?" he asked, cocking his head at it.

"Um, maybe just a hair."

"I'll fix it later. I got the fabric at Babyland."

"You went to Babyland?" she asked, incredulous that her husband had visited the new store on main street.

"Why so surprised?"

"It hardly seems like a place the state's most consulted expert on homicide would hang out. Or the new deputy chief. There's probably some kind of cop rule against it. You are going to be teased unmercifully."

"Just don't tell your big-mouth friend, Candy, or Bradley Moore will be calling for the inside scoop on the new deputy chief. Could you hand me that wrench?"

She wandered back over, handed it to him. "Oliver?"

"Huh?"

"Are we going to the parade tomorrow?"

"Oh, yeah. The parade, the picnic, the fire-works." He slid a look at her. "Are you disap-pointed by the new format?"

This year by unanimous vote, Summer Fest had been made a one-day event, all on the Fourth of July.

"No," Sarah said. "I know the four days just cost too much money, and it was too hard to get volunteers to run all the events. I know my great idea was given a fair trial, two years in a row, and it didn't even come close to saving the town, Oliver. You don't have to be gentle with me."

"Ah, Sarah, you still saved the town."

"I did not!"

But she had saved *him*. Somehow, inside her-self she had found the courage to rescue Oliver Sullivan. Maybe even in a larger world, in the bigger picture, she had only thought she was res-cuing the town, that thought leading her to where she really needed to be.

"I don't know," Oliver said. "When you sold

out Jelly Jeans and Jammies to Smackers and they bought the old factory on Mill Street, they brought a lot of work and money to this town. Eighty employees, at last count. And you know, those articles you write for *Travel* and *Small Town Charm* do more than their fair share of mentioning Kettle Bend. No wonder we have a Babyland on the main street! No wonder Jonathon is opening an office here."

"And then," she said, "there's our most famous citizen."

Moses gazed at her adoringly, looked like he might come over, and then cast a look at the cat, and decided against it. He flopped his tail again.

Moses still got fan mail, he and Oliver were still asked to do follow-up interviews. That whole incident at the river somehow had captured people's hearts and minds and imaginations.

Why?

Sarah thought it stood for good things happening in a world where currents could take you by surprise and sweep you away. It stood for good coming from bad.

It let the world know there were still men who would sacrifice themselves for those who needed them.

And who had needed Oliver more than her?

That was the most wonderful irony in all of it. She had thought she was rescuing him.

In fact, he had rescued her.

The past two years had been beyond anything she could have ever dreamed for herself. Sarah woke in the morning with a song in her heart.

"I'm the luckiest woman in the world," Sarah said, "that you fell in love with me."

She had his full attention. He did that little thing he did. He took her hand, kissed it and then blew on where his lips had been.

"Oh, you are so wrong. I never fell in love with you, Mrs. Sullivan."

"Fine time to tell me now that you've got me knocked up," she teased. She loved more than anything else these moments between them. Ordinary, but not ordinary. The best moments of all. When it seemed like nothing was happening, and yet everything was.

"Love isn't something you fall into," Oliver said, letting go of her hand and eyeing the instructions. He frowned at the crib panel that was definitely on upside down, and possibly backward, too.

He abandoned it suddenly, got up, swept her into his arms and kissed her until she couldn't breathe. Then, looking deep into her eyes, he said, "Love is a choice. It's a daily choice of how to live."

Live love.

He rested his hand on her stomach. There wasn't even a baby bump there yet. She touched his face, relaxed against him, and was sure she felt the new life stir within her.

There was a pure exhilaration in the simplicity of the shared moment that rose within her, and headed like an arrow into the dazzling future.

* * * * *